London's Burning

London's Burning

John Burke

A **London's Burning** Book in association with **LWT**

S I M O N & S C H U S T E R

LONDON·SYDNEY·NEW YORK·TOKYO·SINGAPORE·TORONTO

A London's Burning Book in association with LWT
Based on the original screenplays by
Anita Bronson and Tony Hoare
Series Producer Paul Knight
The London's Burning series is based upon an original film by
Jack Rosenthal
Jacket photograph reproduced by kind permission of LWT

The moral right of the author has been asserted

First published in Great Britain by
Simon & Schuster Ltd in 1992
A Paramount Communications Company

Simon & Schuster Ltd
West Garden Place
Kendal Street
London W2 2AQ

A CIP catalogue record for this book is
available from the British Library
ISNB 0-671-71756-1

Typeset by Hewer Text Composition Services, Edinburgh
Printed and bound in Great Britain by
Harper Collins Manufacturing Ltd, Glasgow

1

IN THE middle of the morning a boy came running along the street. He stopped at a corner, looked from side to side at the traffic, and made a wild dash to the far pavement. For a moment he hesitated, afraid he might have lost his way. His name was David Spence. He was seven years of age, he was almost out of breath, and he was very scared.

When he reached the end of the street he found enough breath for a gasp of relief. Facing him was Blackwall Fire Station. He broke into a last, desperate sprint.

Inside the station, behind the bright red swagger of the two waiting appliances which were drawn up like curry-combed horses gleaming and ready for the off, it had been an uneventful morning so far. Station Officer Tate was taking the opportunity to catch up on some form-filling. He was waiting for the day – and it surely wouldn't be long in coming – when the Watch would be called out on a shout to rescue a station officer from beneath an avalanche of paperwork.

His sub officer, John Hallam, put his head round the door and then hastily retreated. Tate allowed himself a dour grin. Hallam knew when to keep a low profile, and any time the guv'nor was involved in this sort of thing it was best to keep the profile very low indeed.

Tate looked at his watch for the tenth time in one hour. There was still most of the day to go; hour after hour before he could go home and pour himself a whisky and forget this dump. Only he wouldn't be able forget it. The job stayed with him all the time, nagging at him; and the moment he reached for the bottle, Nancy would be ready to nag if he poured himself too large a measure. They were getting larger by the week, he had to admit it. Wearily he began ticking off the inventory and jotting down notes for the requisitions.

Along the corridor a door slammed and somebody shouted something aggressive: another petty squabble blowing up out of the tedium. When a waiting period grew too long, the Blue Watch team soon tired of reading or playing snooker. Charisma might be content to finger through the pages of girlie magazines and surreptitiously study Lonely Hearts ads, thinking nobody noticed, but the rest of them had a lower doldrums threshold. It wasn't that they wanted to spend every minute of the day risking their lives, but when they weren't in action, the strain was almost worse. Boredom had to be alleviated by bitchiness. The station officer had more than once noticed the disbelieving curl of Josie Ingham's lips: Josie, the only woman in the Watch, was no match for the men when it came to gossip and snide needling. Repetitive, rambling insults were as much a part of the station routine as cleaning and checking and re-checking the apparatus.

Tate's pen poised over a list of spare parts. Had Vaseline remembered to follow up that business of the faulty clutch?

That was another thing: the nicknames the men bestowed on one another. They were like schoolkids, doing a sort of playground 'Yah-boo, fatty' at other kids they saw too often, for too long, each day. Mike Wilson had been dubbed Bayleaf because he was mess manager. Moon-faced Leslie Appleby had become Charisma for the simple reason that that was exactly what he lacked. As for Vaseline . . . Tate had never fathomed why

6

Roland Cartwright should have acquired that title, though it might have had something to do with him being a bit of a slippery customer. No doubt his first two wives would have had something to say about that. He had not been married long enough to the third one for her to complain too loudly – not yet.

Tate turned his attention dismally to the fuel return and a query from the powers-that-be about the average consumption by the pump ladder vehicle.

There was a sudden shout from the direction of the Watch room, accompanied by an odd, piping little voice which could not belong to any of the men on the team, unless maybe one had trapped part of his anatomy in the turntable ladder.

Tate was glad of an excuse to abandon the paperwork and go to the Watch room. Sicknote, an expert at providing medical evidence of unfitness for work, was trying to calm an agitated little boy who was wailing, 'She's on the roof . . . my gran . . . can't get down . . .'

'Hold on, son, hold on. Get your breath back.'

Two minutes later the nattering and needling had ceased, giving way to the two-tone howl of one of the appliances echoing along the street. Vaseline was driving as fast as he dared through the mid-morning traffic and pedestrians. Station Officer Tate sat beside him, while little David Spence stood behind, held firmly by George Green. It was pretty heady stuff for a kid. He was still worried stiff, but couldn't help gasping with excitement as they slewed round a corner and the bray of the siren echoed back from a block of flats.

'Where next, son?'

'Down here . . . there, the street at the end. You *will* save her, won't you, mister?'

'Don't you worry,' said Tate confidently. 'Now, how old is this friend of yours?'

'My gran says she's a year older than me.'

'And how old are you?'

'Seven and a quarter.'

Tate pursed his lips. He didn't like the sound of this. A scared eight-year-old girl up on a roof could really pose a problem if she went and panicked before they could get close. As to how she had been allowed to get up there in the first place . . .

David added: 'My gran got her when she was a kitten.'

Vaseline came close to giving his nickname a new connotation when he let the appliance slither to one side for a moment. He regained control, and slowed down before the house at which David was pointing.

The cat was a small tabby, crouching in the lee of a chimney stack, emitting the occasional pitiful miaow. An elderly lady peering upwards from the front gate turned to greet the firemen and put her arm round David's shoulders.

'I'm sorry, officer. He just ran off before I could stop him. I'd no idea where he was going. But he's so fond of Beatrice. He does love her. We both do.'

The two of them stared pleadingly upwards as the ladder began to swing into position. George Green went up, making stupid noises which he supposed to be friendly cat language. The animal watched him dubiously, but made no move to scuttle off along the ridge of the roof. From this angle it was obvious how the animal had got up there: branches of a tree, too large for such a small garden, had sagged towards the gable end and were scraping the slates. They would have supported the weight of a cat, but not any human rescuer who tried to clamber up that way.

The ladder platform was poised above the slates. George reached out, got a grip, and brought the cat

8

slowly and safely down to ground level. David clutched it close to him.

'Tell you what, love,' Tate said to the old lady, as Vaseline climbed back into the driver's seat and began reversing the appliance in a slow arc so that he could be ready to head back to the station, 'I'll see if I can get one of the lads round to chop a bit of that tree down. Stop her shinning over on to the roof again.' He reached out and ruffled David's hair. 'All okay now, then?'

David squeezed the cat ecstatically. It wriggled and suddenly shot from his arms. There was a scurry of paws, and then one brief scream from the boy. It had gone straight under the nearside wheel of the pump ladder which had rescued it.

There was a bleak silence in the cab as the appliance made its way back through the streets, a lot more slowly than it had come.

'Well,' said Vaseline defensively, 'it wasn't my fault.'

'Cat killer,' said Charisma from behind.

'Certainly the crudest form of vivisection,' added Malcolm Cross in that lofty, intolerably condescending tone of his.

'I don't believe this.' Vaseline could not be sure whether or not they were winding him up. 'How was I supposed to know it was going to do that? I mean, it was a suicidal cat from the start. Why else was it on the roof? This was probably its tenth try. It had blown the allotted nine lives. Definitely suicide.'

'Has a certain crass logic to it, I suppose,' Malcolm conceded.

Vaseline leaned over the wheel in sullen silence, then tensed and straightened up. A middle-aged man had emerged from the public convenience at the road junction ahead and was waving, looking as if he might at any moment blunder out into the road. Vaseline had

had more than enough of squashing things under his wheels for one day. He slowed down and stopped.

The pasty-faced man who had flagged them down was in a state of some distress, compulsively plucking at the corner of his mouth with his right hand and waving his left hand back towards the toilet block. His dark-blue business suit was rumpled, the jacket lopsided as if he had been trying vainly to tug it into shape over his shoulders.

'Oh God, please . . . p-please help!' His voice was a high-pitched whine. 'I think he may be dying. I think they may have drowned him.'

Tate glanced back over his shoulder. 'Charisma, get the Brooks airway and call an ambulance.' He lowered himself on to the pavement. 'Try and calm down, sir. Just show us where, all right, Mr . . . er . . .?'

'Briant. It was dreadful, dreadful! Two vicious hooligans, out of nowhere.'

'Easy, Mr Briant.' Tate led the way into the toilet. There was nobody else in sight.

'Pushing his head down, flushing it. I couldn't do anything,' Briant was babbling. 'There – over there.'

In one of the cubicles the crumpled shape of a man was propped against the toilet bowl. His head and shoulders were soaking wet and blood was seeping from his upper lip. At a nod from Tate, Josie and Vaseline half-lifted, half-dragged him out on to the main floor.

'He's not dead, is he?' Briant clutched his head and looked as if he might pass out or throw up. 'I couldn't bear it.'

Malcolm caught Josie's eye as she straightened up and made a limp-wristed gesture. They turned the man face down. It looked as if he had swallowed a fair quantity of water. Tate kneeled astride him and began to apply artificial respiration. After three powerful presses on the lungs, he expelled a rush of water on to the slimy floor.

10

Charisma appeared in the doorway. 'It's gone. It ain't there.'

'What isn't?'

'The Brooks airway. Those bastards from S.W. Division must've nicked it when we was on that shout with them yesterday.'

Tate wondered bitterly how many times he had told the team to check every bit of equipment after a shout with other areas. Later he would raise the subject yet again. Right now he went on pumping away at the prone figure on the floor.

Very quietly, but with impeccable clarity, Malcolm said: 'Looks like a case of queer-bashing.'

Briant edged a few feet towards the wall of the end cubicle, pretending not to hear.

'That's enough of that, Leading Fireman Cross.' Tate waved Vaseline and Charisma to bend down and roll the man over, face up. 'Let's try mouth-to-mouth.'

There was a pause. Everybody was looking away in a different direction.

'Well, come on, then,' growled Tate. 'You, Cartwright.'

Vaseline blenched. 'Well, I . . . actually, Malc's better at it than me, guv.'

'Nonsense,' said Malcolm quickly. 'Charisma's better at it than any of us.'

'No I'm not!'

Tate shrugged contemptuously, and bent down to tackle the job himself.

'Guv, do you think it's wise?' said Malcolm. He made a discreet nod in Briant's direction. 'I mean, the cut lip, you know.'

'Union's against it – the kiss of life in cases like this,' added Charisma.

Josie, who rarely had cause to spend much time in a gents' lavatory, was glancing curiously around. She

11

handed Tate a clean handkerchief. He wiped the blood from the man's mouth. 'Somebody go and keep an eye out for the ambulance.'

Malcolm, Vaseline and Charisma all moved as one man towards the exit.

'Stay here!' roared Tate. He nodded at Josie. 'You go. And you'd better raise a police unit as well.'

Briant, who had been fidgeting unhappily, lunged forward to block Josie's way out.

'I . . . look, excuse me, but is it absolutely essential to involve the police?' He glanced down at the prone figure and then looked hastily away again. 'I mean, he just needs medical attention, doesn't he?'

Malcolm said with a certain sadistic pleasure: 'If he dies, it'll be a murder enquiry.'

At that moment the man on the floor coughed and retched and tried to turn his head. There was a mutter of relief all round.

'Still want me to call in the police, guv?' asked Josie.

'That's the procedure, Ingham.' Aware of Briant's pleading look, Tate snapped: 'You do want the people responsible for this to get caught, don't you?'

Briant gave the distinct impression of wishing he had never summoned help in the first place. 'Well, yes, of course. Only, it's all rather embarrassing. The fact is I have this rather sensitive job.'

Tate wavered. 'Well, I don't know, sir.'

'I mean, it's not as if I even know this person. I just happened to be here, and – '

'What's happened?' It was a bewildered croak from the man on the floor, trying to push himself up and looking straight at Briant.

'You do understand, don't you?' Briant appealed to the others.

'Oh, we understand.'

12

'Definitely.'

'The Ambulance Union's also against it, as well you know,' said Charisma earnestly. 'Kiss of life, in a case like this, very dodgy.'

Tate glared. 'You ever considered joining the diplomatic service, Appleby?'

They ate late before settling back into the routine of boredom and bickering. Station Officer Tate resumed his own sort of boredom, digging down into the pile of paperwork until he came across a schedule buried in its depths. Here was something that had been well and truly overlooked. Best to clear it up quickly, before some Divisional busybody started asking questions. At least it would get him out of the building again. He reached for the phone and announced himself and his intentions rather more curtly than he would have done normally. He got a sadistic pleasure from hearing the twitter of panic which his call had provoked at the other end.

'I don't understand what it is you are saying. What is this fire inspection?'

'The fire brigade, Mr Malik, has an obligation under Section 11D of the Fire Services Act for us to familiarize ourselves with any public premises, should they ever have a fire.'

'All precautions are taken,' came a plaintive, sing-song protest. 'I have never had a fire. All precautions are taken, you have my word.'

'Nevertheless, sir, we do have a legal duty to make regular inspections of premises such as yours. Perhaps we may pay you a courtesy call in about half an hour?'

When the voice of indignation and apprehension at the other end of the line had finished speaking, he hung up and walked along to the Watch room. 'Leading Fireman Cross. Firewoman Ingham.'

'Guv?'

'I've decided it's time to call on Mr Malik. Should have done it weeks ago.'

'Mr who?'

'Malik. Of Malik Fabrics, behind the dock road. You two come along with me. Keep you from falling asleep. I've told him we're on our way.'

'Doesn't give him much warning, guv.'

'That's precisely the idea.'

Although it was a matter of form to make grimaces of disgust at the prospect of work, Tate could see that Malcolm Cross, like himself, was really not too unhappy to be out of the station for a while. Cross was a bit toffee-nosed and disdained to share in the familiar jokes and insults. Neither could he summon up even a pretence of tolerance towards the amorous exploits or non-exploits of his mates: Bayleaf with some hushed-up troubles at home; Josie Ingham mooning about because of a no-good husband who kept disappearing, coming back and then disappearing again; and Vaseline, newly-launched on his third wife and boasting about what happened within two minutes of his getting home off watch duty. Definitely not to Cross's refined tastes.

The building looked unprepossessing from the outside, with brickwork that bore all the signs of having been damaged in World War II and never repaired. The pavement near the entrance had a number of dangerous cracks in it, and two neighbouring warehouses had been abandoned long ago, their shattered windows boarded up.

It didn't look much better inside, and the noise was overpowering. The workshop was packed with sewing machines and rolls of material, cartons of buttons and zips, with almost no visible floor space. Light bulbs were strung out in a continuous wire hanging from loops

14

pinned to the ceiling, shining down on the dark heads of Indian girls working away at the machines.

Mr Malik saw them from his little office and came out, squeezing across the cluttered aisle and offering Tate a wide, insincere smile. Fussily he began a conducted tour, talking over his shoulder or across a machine when they got separated. Very little of what he was saying made much sense above the din of the machines.

Finally Tate, exasperated, called a halt. He rattled the bar of a door and pointed to the sign above it. 'You see what it says, Mr Malik? Fire Exit.'

'That is right, that is precisely what it is for, sir.'

Tate indicated the chain and padlock securing the door. 'So why is it padlocked?'

'We have had many burglaries, you understand.'

'During working hours, Mr Malik?'

'Ah, that is the insurance company, I'm afraid.' Malik looked pleased with his own swiftness. 'They insist on security precautions.'

'Not this kind, they don't,' said Tate grimly.

He sent Josie to check the fire extinguishers and the light switches. It came as no surprise that all four extinguishers were way out of date. Malcolm Cross began examining the windows, one of which had a catch so rusted and immovable that it had obviously not been opened for months, maybe years. Nor, for that matter, had the panes ever been cleaned, and the grease on them and on some of the machines would burn beautifully if ever a fire got hold.

After a few minutes Tate noticed that Cross was stopping rather a long time beside one window, yet wasn't paying much attention to the window itself. Close to it was a rack on which completed work was hung. A slim Asian girl was adding a few garments. Her own clothes, unlike those of most of the other operatives, were westernized. As she turned away, she bumped into Malcolm. Tate got the impression that the leading fireman had been moving into position to ensure that the accident would take place.

As the racket of the machines abated, with the operatives cautiously watching Mr Malik and the newcomers, Tate caught a few snatches of conversation between Malcolm and the girl.

'How do you stand it in here?'

'Better than the streets of Calcutta.'

'Is that where you come from – Calcutta?'

'Born and bred in Bethnal Green.'

The two of them laughed. She was very pretty, quite out of place in this sordid sweatshop. She had a fine, dignified poise, the movement of her arms graceful and assured as she moved the clothes along the rail. But her dark eyes were shy, seeming to recede into secret depths when anyone looked directly at her.

Tate growled: 'Leading Fireman Cross – go and have a look at that stairway at the end.'

'Right, guv.'

He was back in a matter of minutes, by means of a detour which took him close to the girl again.

He said: 'There's a whole pile of boxes half-way down, guv. No way of getting past them if there was an emergency.'

Tate glared at Malik.

'I assure you, officer' – Malik was oozing sincerity – 'on my word, the boxes will be moved today. They have only just been delivered.'

'So far, Mr Malik, I calculate eight serious violations.'

Malcolm Cross leaned forward and abruptly launched into a language of which Tate did not understand a word. Malik all too clearly understood every single one, and flinched.

'What lingo is that?' Tate demanded.

16

'Punjabi,' said Cross loftily. 'Funnily enough' – he raised his voice for the benefit of the girl by the clothes rack – '*I* was born in India, and I've just been telling our friend here that you have the authority to have this place shut down double-quick unless regulations are strictly enforced.'

'Hidden talents, eh?' Tate grunted.

'Just so, guv. Perfect senior officer material, I would suggest.'

'What you can suggest right now is that Mr Malik here had better get his act together within the next forty-eight hours. A fire prevention officer will be paying a visit to check that everything's been done.'

As they left, Josie said amiably: 'Very attractive, Malc.'

'You think so?'

'I think *you* thought so.'

Malcolm shrugged. 'I was interested in her background. A pity that an intelligent girl like that has to slog away in such a dump. Not much better than slavery.'

'Almost as bad as the fire service?'

Tate repressed the urge to snarl at the two of them and demand more respect for the Service. He was wondering, not for the first time, whether it really deserved any, which was no way for a man in his position to be thinking.

The gearbox gave out an unpleasant grinding noise on a sharp corner. George Green, who was at the wheel, said: 'There's definitely something dicey in there but it's damned intermittent. Can't trace it.' The noise ceased and they went along at the usual pace without further trouble. Over his shoulder George said: 'Just what was all that jabbering about, Malc? Telling him Indian speaks with forked tongue?'

'Actually,' said Malcolm with dignity, 'I told him we

could have him closed down in a matter of days.' He looked at the station officer for a hint of approval.

Tate snorted. 'More like bloody weeks, the time it takes to get a magistrate to authorize a prohibition notice nowadays.'

As they went into the station, Bayleaf came out of the kitchen and glanced at Josie. 'Welcome back to the madhouse. How's life treating you?'

'About the same way as a baby treats a nappy.' Josie shot him a brief smile, then caught Tate's eye and looked away.

He sighed. If there was one thing he liked to avoid more than any other in the ranks, it was marital, or ex-marital, trouble. There were enough sour jokes going the rounds among the men's wives about the one woman in the Watch. Even his own wife had clumsily tried to suggest that he was not immune to Josie's charms. Pathetic – really Nancy should know better – but women couldn't resist hinting and speculating.

Maybe something was beginning to brew between Josie and Bayleaf. Both of them were vulnerable right now, with domestic problems in each of their lives. Tate went back to his office and hoped to God that he wouldn't find himself having to expand the paperwork with official reports on a scandal in the station.

As for his own marital bliss, he found himself wondering whether Nancy might just happen to be out at the supermarket when he got home, or on the phone to her mother or sister or somebody – anybody – so that he could get a quick drink in without her noticing.

2

Tony Sanderson braced himself. He could tell from his wife's expression that she was longing to find an excuse not to come with him this morning. Slumped on the edge of the bed, she managed to look depressed and stubborn at the same time. Before he could utter a word she said: 'I don't want to go.'

'But I told them you was going.' Gently he lifted her to her feet. 'Come on, D. Please.'

'Why? I just don't want to.'

He hesitated, then risked it: 'I want you where I can keep my eyes on you. In case you want to go shopping again.' When she winced, he kissed her and put his dark brown hand affectionately against her pale white cheek. 'Come on, D, it's for a good cause.'

There had been a brief spell when they had nick-named him Token, as the token black on the team. Then they had switched to calling him Tone. It was not that Tony minded the 'token' reference: he was good-humoured about anything of that kind. But somehow the others felt uneasy and it was tacitly agreed to drop the name.

What he had still not learned to be good-humoured about were the looks and muttered remarks that often followed them when he was out with his wife – his white wife. He knew it affected Dorothy, too. That was one reason why she didn't want to come out with the team today. A Sunday afternoon walk in the park was one thing; you didn't have to speak to people, you could look straight ahead, pass their sneering faces and go on your way. A whole morning parading up and down the main shopping streets in his company, actually approaching people rather than dodging away from them, was a very different thing.

But Dorothy was going to come. He had told the Blue Watch team that she would be there to lend a hand like the other wives, and she would have to go along with him.

The Watch was on night shift, but every member was giving up one day for a charity collection. A kid crippled in a car accident had lost his whole family and would need special steel braces if he was ever to walk again. Members of the Watch had dug him out of the wreckage. You weren't supposed to feel any personal ties with people you had rescued – there were too many of them, and you'd be no good as a firefighter if you got emotionally involved with each and every one – but there was something about this particular kid that had hit all of them. The fact that the local divisional officer had approvingly said it would be good publicity for the fire brigade had almost put them off at one stage. That hadn't been the idea behind it at all. But they stuck to their original motive for the cause, and to hell with the D.O.'s public relations angle.

Market day was obviously the best one for the collection. The shopping precinct provided an ideal arena for a demonstration of the old manual pump they had borrowed from the museum, and the congestion of market stalls at the southern end of the street made it difficult for potential contributors to escape from the rattle and swing of the collecting buckets.

When a sufficiently large crowd had gathered to find out what was going on, Malcolm Cross took charge. It was not often that he had the chance of bellowing orders to Station Officer Tate and Sub Officer Hallam. Along with Vaseline and Sicknote they began manhandling the pump from its trailer. 'Not so much as a scratch!' pleaded Malcolm, who had personally signed for the historic piece of equipment.

As Tony steered the reluctant Dorothy towards the group, he noted that Charisma was hanging back in a doorway, determined not to get involved in any physical effort more demanding than carrying a collecting bucket.

'Hello, you lot.' Malcolm turned his attention to the newcomers, enjoying handing out another batch of orders. 'See George. He'll supply you with T-shirts. That shop down the road printed the Alan Aldridge Appeal slogan for us. Also get yourself a bucket or helmet to collect contributions.'

'Who's doing the pushing and who the collecting, then?' asked Tony.

'This is a democratic country, Tone. Straws will be drawn.'

'I do beg your pardon, Malc. Hadn't realized democracy's defined by straws.'

Dorothy tugged unhappily at his arm, embarrassed by any snide remarks which to her seemed to be leading up to a row. She was unused to the joshing that always went on amongst them.

Tony was grateful to Josie for picking up the vibes. 'Take no notice, love, they're all idiots.'

A fire brigade car appeared suddenly at the end of the precinct opening on to the main road. Two uniformed officers climbed out, one with a camera. Close at hand was an obvious press photographer. The D.O. had personally made sure that the publicity element was not going to be neglected.

The parade was ready to move off. With five of them pushing, two on either side and one at the back, the pump began to creak on its way. There was a splutter of cheering from the spectators. Then, before they could disperse, the rest of the Watch were among them, thrusting red buckets and yellow helmets under their noses.

With his shoulder to the back of the pump, Tony caught the occasional glimpse of Dorothy. She was too shy to make a good collector. She held a helmet out tentatively, but could not be brash and pushy enough. The third time he looked in her direction she had been distracted by something in a shop window. Tony groaned. It was her fatal weakness. He loved her, God how he loved her, but one day it would bring them both down, this affliction of hers.

By mid-afternoon they had had enough. Heading for the nearest pub, Blue Watch monopolized the quietest corner – at least it had been quiet until now. Tate politely offered Dorothy a drink before they started counting up the proceeds but she shook her head, whispered an awkward, 'No, thanks a lot', and handed over the helmet with some loose change clinking about inside. Clutching Tony's arm, she said: 'Can we go now?'

'Don't you want to see how much we've made?'

'Not 'specially. I'd like to get back.'

'Look, I've got to stay and have a drink with the lads.'

'You stay, then.' She was not complaining, simply eager to be out of the pub door and away. 'I'll see you back home. Get you something to eat.'

He put his arm round her and squeezed her. 'Straight home, mind.'

Her shoulder flinched within his grasp. Then she forced a smile and left.

Tate and Hallam settled at a table and began counting the money. It came to 'One thousand, two hundred and thirty-four quid, and forty-eight pee'. There was a cheer which startled an elderly alcoholic at the far end of the bar into choking over his whisky.

'It's a lot of change.' Josie peered at the mounds of coppers and small silver.

'That's all right,' said Tate. 'The bank on the corner said they'd switch it into notes for us.' He turned to his sub officer. 'Want to give me a hand with this? We'll get it papered up and then I'll stick it in the station. Too late to bank it.'

'Hardly worth it, anyway,' said Hallam, 'if we're going to make the presentation on Saturday. That was the idea, wasn't it?'

'It was, and still is.'

There was a rush to order celebratory drinks at the bar. Bayleaf was carrying a glass towards Josie, edging a few feet away from the others. George Green turned to offer Tony a pint, but Tony was suddenly as anxious to get away as Dorothy had been. Straight home, he had warned her. Could he be sure she had done what he had asked?

He tried to tell himself it would be all right. After that last spate they had had, she was cured. Had to be. She wouldn't let him down by doing anything so stupid again. She had promised.

When he let himself into the flat he was longing desperately for her to be there, standing at the stove, ready to turn and hold her arms out to him. But there was nobody. She had not been back, he could tell. It ought not to have taken her that long to pick up a few things for supper.

Just as he turned, wondering whether to storm out in search of her, there was the scrape of her key in the lock. She came in, trying to take out the key without dropping the shopping bags festooned around her arms.

She stared, letting go of a plastic holdall. 'Tony, I

23

didn't expect . . . I mean, I didn't think you'd have finished so soon.'

He picked up the holdall and looked inside. There was a new mantelpiece clock on the top, with a couple of small cushions below. And what the hell would he find in the other bags?

Before he could say a word she was already sobbing, chucking everything aside and dashing into the sitting-room to throw herself on the settee. He grabbed two of the shopping bags at random and followed her. When he tipped the contents on to the floor, it was all pretty well what he had expected: a menagerie of china animals, yet another small mirror, and two candlesticks. And of all things she had bought a brass fireside companion set – even though they had an electric fire.

'Look at it!' He waved helplessly at the knick-knacks on the wall-hung shelving and the narrow mantelpiece. 'I mean, just take a look. It's lunacy. It looks like . . . I dunno . . . a bloody bring-and-buy sale. It's got to stop, it's simply *got* to stop!'

And hardly any of it paid for, he raged inwardly. It was an illness. How could she go on like this? How did she expect them ever to pay for all this rubbish? Tony dragged open a top drawer in the sideboard and dug out a sheaf of letters and bills, thrusting them under Dorothy's nose. More bills than Parliament ever got! Bills from lawyers, debt collecting agencies, bills, more bills . . .

'I'm a bloody fireman,' he yelled, 'not a financial tycoon!' He snatched up the handbag she had dropped on the settee beside her and opened it. Two department store credit cards jutted up from an inner side pocket. 'I just can't believe it. How can you keep getting these things? I thought they had computers . . . blacklists . . . Dorothy, *how*?'

She raised her head at last. Her ashen cheeks were

smeared with tears, tinted with the heavy blue eye-liner which always made her look bruised and melancholy. 'I just . . . I fill out a form and they . . . well, they send them. It's not my fault.'

'Then whose bloody fault is it?'

'They make it so easy,' she sobbed.

He tried to tear the credit cards across. He had strong fingers, but they were not up to the task. The deadly cards refused to be destroyed.

One thing about being on night shift or on rest days was that you had a chance of making some spare cash: moonlighting by daylight, you might say. It was frowned on by the top brass, but then, the top brass didn't need spare brass as much as the ordinary fireman did. George Green, with no wife at home to insist that he spend his spare time with her, was glad of the chance of driving a hire car for his brother-in-law. Vaseline, with a new wife at home and repeated demands from his two discarded wives, specialized in local gardening jobs, but was prepared to turn his hand to anything that resulted in cash drifting his way.

Marion Cartwright was one of those wives who was in favour of the husband spending a lot of time with her and taking her out. She was suspicious of his latest gardening venture.

'I'm not like the other two, you know.' Her bright red lips could be enticing when she was greedy for him to come to bed. They could also produce a heavy, aggressive pout. Right now they were pouting. 'I won't put up with it.'

'Put up with what?'

'You messing around with other women.'

'That's funny. I don't remember you having any moral objections to *us* messing around while I was still married to my last wife.'

'You can be a real pig, d'you know that?'

He slid his hand inside her blouse and fondled her, snuggling his face into her neck. She giggled and tried to push him away.

'I want your body.' He pressed her against the wall. 'Now!'

'Roland . . .'

It delayed his departure for the gardening job by fifteen minutes. Marion seemed content to let him go now, having made sure he was in no state to satisfy any other woman for a while to come.

At the door she watched him tying his fireman's boots to the back of his bike. 'You once told me it wasn't allowed.'

'What isn't allowed?'

'Wearing your boots for other jobs.'

'Well, I like to live dangerously, don't I?'

He set off for the neglected garden of Mrs Simms, and for the money that would slip into his pocket by that evening.

By early evening, George Green had been to and from Heathrow twice, collected a cantankerous old woman from a funeral cold buffet, and had a brief argument with a drunken client who claimed that he had been overcharged and taken by an unnecessarily roundabout route. The argument was brief because the man sobered up enough, just in time, to get George's face into focus. Nobody had ever given George a nickname. Once an amateur boxer, he had suffered a badly bashed nose which surely invited the bestowal of some sort of flippant name. But one look at that nose and at George's brooding face, and most people decided that discretion was the better part of valour. The passenger took that one look, and paid up.

Then came the big surprise of the day. George was sitting in the office, with half an hour to spare before

26

picking up some punters from the theatre, when the phone rang. He picked it up and heard a familiar voice, but he could not quite believe what it was saying.

'Me and my bird,' Charisma declared airily, 'need to get back to her place. I thought, you know, I could put the fare your way. I'm sure she'd like to meet you, anyway. I've told her what big mates we are, and all that.'

'What is this, Charisma – a wind-up?'

'No, straight. We're in the Indian down Archibald Street, not far from the station. You know the one.'

'Yes, I know.'

'It won't take long.'

George glanced at the wall clock. He supposed he could just fit in the trip, and he really did have to see this: Charisma, with a bird? She must be a pretty desperate drag to be seen with someone as feeble as Leslie Appleby.

When the two emerged from the restaurant he could not believe his eyes. The girl was tall, slim and elegant, and as she stooped to climb into the back of the car her coat hung loose and he saw the shape underneath her dress within, swelling much too appetizingly for anyone like Charisma to appreciate. Charisma, thought George uncharitably, must be paying her. But you'd need to do a lot of moonlighting to raise the cash to pay someone of that class.

'You all right?' In his mirror he could see the glint on her knee as she crossed her legs.

'Nicola,' said Charisma cockily, 'this is George.' It dawned on George that Charisma had called him rather than any other driver because he wanted word to get around the station about his stunning bit of stuff. 'George – Nicola McQueen.'

'Right.' George was still awestruck. 'And you want to be dropped off where?'

'Er . . .'

'Clissold Avenue,' said Nicola throatily. 'Number twenty-six.'

'And on the way,' said Charisma, 'd'you mind if we just drop in to the station? There's something I forgot.' He leaned back and let his arm stray around Nicola's shoulders. 'Red Watch is on tonight. Don Farmer's the guv'nor – good mate of mine. Shame we won't have time to show you round.'

George Green rolled his eyes disbelievingly towards the heavens.

When he put Charisma down at the station, wondering what on earth he could want from inside when he had a date like this ready and waiting outside, there was a long silence. Then Nicola said in that faintly hoarse voice of hers: 'It must be quite exciting, being a fireman.'

'It has its moments.' George could not resist the question: 'How did you come to meet Charisma?'

'Charisma?'

'That's his nickname. Most of us have them in this service.'

'He . . . didn't tell you how the two of us got together, then?'

'No. Not exactly.' He waited for an explanation; but in vain.

When Charisma returned he was carrying a half-filled plastic sack. Its contents were something George would also have liked to ask about; but he had a feeling that this was not the evening when he would get any rational answers. He went on wondering just how Charisma was going to cope with this incredible bird.

Charisma didn't know quite what the ravishing Nicola had in mind, but he had a feeling that it was going to be exciting. A bit odd, in a way, wanting him to dress up in his full fireman's gear rather than wanting him to get stripped off ready for action. But if that was what gave her a kick, fine. She was waiting in her bedroom, and he wasn't going to disappoint her . . . he hoped.

It was all a bit breathtaking. Charisma took a deep gulp to get some of that breath back, and then tapped on the bedroom door.

'Nicola. I'm ready.'

'Just a moment.' There was a throbbing pause, and then, 'You can come in now.'

Charisma drew himself up to his full height, put his helmet on, and strode in.

He had one glimpse of Nicola in suspenders and stockings and a few wisps of something flimsy which concealed nothing. He took another happy, hopeful pace into the bedroom before being half-blinded by a camera flash. As he blinked, Nicola put the camera reverently down on her bed and came close up to him. She pressed herself against his belt and buttons, and her breathing quickened. Just as he was fumbling to undo the belt, she gave a little shudder and pushed herself away.

'No, it's no good.'

'What's no good?'

'I'm sorry, Leslie. This must end now, before it goes any further.'

'Now just a minute, what the . . .'

His voice trailed away. Over her sweet-smelling shoulder he saw the wall of the room beside the bed. It was covered with framed photographs of men in different uniforms: a soldier, a policeman, a traffic warden, a sailor, even a hotel doorman. The face in each picture bore the same expression of bemusement Charisma must have shown when the flash went off in his face.

'Now go,' said Nicola tragically.

Before he could summon up the energy to argue, she took him by the shoulders, turned him briskly around, and thrust him towards the sitting-room. She stayed in the bedroom with the door locked until he had changed back into his civvies again, then came out and opened the front door of the flat for him as if he had just read the gas meter. Maybe there was indeed a photograph in that room of hers of a meter reader. The front door clicked tidily shut behind him.

He stumped wretchedly homewards. The woman must be a nut-case. Surely there was some way of suing that Lonely Hearts magazine? Advertising under false pretences . . . Trades Descriptions Act, or something. And what the hell was he going to tell George Green in the morning?

He was on his own doorstep before it dawned on him that he need make no excuses to George or any of the others. George had seen Nicola and had dropped them at her flat. He had had a good look at Nicola and what she was made of. What had happened after that was something Charisma would happily wipe from his mind; but there was no harm in George and the boys indulging their own imaginations.

After a nearly sleepless night he reached the station in tolerably good humour.

Vaseline had just arrived with his fireman's boots under his arm. Malcolm Cross looked disapprovingly at them and muttered: 'Unofficial use of, eh? Naughty.'

Any excuses Vaseline might have wanted to offer were overridden by George Green's welcome to Charisma. 'Last to arrive – whacked out from screwing?'

Charisma shrugged, pleased with the way they were staring at him. 'Oh, I suppose you had to tell everyone, did you?'

'Too right. It's a total mystery to me.'

30

'Take no notice,' said Josie. 'He's only jealous.'

'All right, all right.' George could not take his eyes off Charisma. 'Come on, tell us where you met her?'

Charisma was loving every minute of this. He tried to look offhand. 'We just sort of bumped into each other in this, uh, wine bar.'

'Wine bar? *You?*'

'Yeah. And, well, we just got chatting. Natural affinity thing, you know.'

Vaseline looked as if he wanted to say something but could not summon up the words. It was rare for all of them to be so utterly stumped.

'Only trouble is' – Charisma could not stop himself now – 'she's very demanding. Know what I mean? You have to be extra fit with a woman like Nicola.' He tried a compassionate smile on Sicknote. 'No good for someone like you – not with that bad back of yours.'

'God,' said Josie remotely. 'Men!'

It was promising to turn into an uneventful morning, which gave them more time to concentrate on Charisma and this strange creature which they all would have believed was a creation of his own wish-fulfilment if it had not been for George's testimony. Charisma was in no hurry for it to stop.

Then the bells went down.

The telex had churned out an address that could hardly be called one as such, referring only to a huddle of abandoned warehouses on the edge of a demolition site. When the two pumps swung round the corner on to a cracked road surface, one derelict building was completely ablaze, watched by two policemen who had reported the outbreak. At least there was plenty of space in which to manoeuvre. Tate and Hallam crackled out orders and Blue Watch went into action as if on a neat training exercise. An ambulance bumped over the uneven surface to position itself beside the police car.

31

Tate stood by one of the policemen. 'There's nobody in there, is there?'

'Can't be sure.'

The other policeman shielded his eyes against a drift of pungent smoke. 'There's an old dosser lives in the basement. Harmless enough, we don't bother him. But if he was smoking a fag and trying to drink his usual dose of meths at the same time . . .'

Tate hurried away. 'Wilson, Quigley, Cross, Ingham . . . get your sets on. Could be somebody in the basement.'

The four of them pulled their breathing apparatus over their faces. Three headed into the inferno. Vaseline made his way along the front of the building, looking for a hatch or flap which might give access to the basement. Heat seared out at him through broken windows. Fire erupted suddenly through a split in the pavement. He stepped warily round it, probing for an entrance somewhere. Inside it was worse: impossible to see any door or any other opening through the writhing smoke. A burning floorboard tilted down from above, bringing a shower of grit and sparks with it. The heat was growing more and more intense. Sicknote and Malcolm Cross hauled the hoses forward, trying to beat the flames down, but the rotten timbers and the accumulation of dust and rubbish were fuelling the blaze faster than it could be thrust back. Josie Ingham dodged a scorching tongue greedy to devour her, and cannoned into a beam which crumpled and added to the conflagration.

In the searing light a flight of steps down into the basement was revealed. Josie hosed a way through embers which had not properly taken hold, and waved to Malcolm to join her. They found the dosser almost immediately – or what was left of him. It was impossible to lift him out: his flesh had melted right through the springs.

All at once Vaseline, outside, let out a scream of anguish. A gap had opened in the wall, and what looked like a trickle of molten lava licked towards his boots. The toecaps immediately caught fire.

'Bloody hell!' Tate grabbed a hose and swung it along the building. 'Hit the deck, son.' He turned the full force of the jet on the blazing boots, while Vaseline whimpered in agony. Steam rose above his feet and swirled around his sobbing curses.

The ambulance, not needed for what was left of the dosser, carried Vaseline off to hospital. The others took twenty minutes to make sure the blaze was well and truly damped down, and made their way back to Blackwall Station. When they had cleared away the apparatus they cleaned themselves up and gathered in the mess around cups of tea.

'I just don't understand it,' said Hallam for the tenth time since they had left the gutted warehouse. 'They just ignited. Went up like that. His *boots*. I mean, it wasn't as if he was standing all that close. Just seemed to go up.'

'Bit worrying, if you think about it,' Malcolm agreed.

Charisma sipped his tea. The subject had changed to everyday matters too readily for his liking. 'Be an enquiry, d'you think?'

'Could well be.'

'He's going to be all right, though, isn't he?' asked Josie.

'Be off work for a bit,' said Hallam. 'Makes a change. Usually Sicknote who gets the doctor's scribble.'

Malcolm looked awkwardly into his teacup, then decided to speak. 'You know he's been using his boots for a spot of moonlighting.'

'That's against regulations.'

'No need to grass,' said George Green.

'I was just trying to – '

33

'I think he just wanted to skive off, so he hot-footed it out of there, you might say.'

There was a groan, cut off as the phone began to ring. Bayleaf answered it. 'Pigsty here.' Then he glanced across the table at George. 'For you. A lady called Nicola. Says you gave her a lift home the other night with . . . uh . . . Leslie.' In the lull of uncertainty he said into the mouthpiece: 'Leslie's here, actually, if you want to speak to him.' He shook his head and held the receiver out to George. 'No, it's you she wants.'

For almost the first time in history there was virtual silence in the mess. Nobody made any pretence of not listening as George mumbled into the phone. 'Well, okay, I guess.' He listened, trying not to look at Charisma, who was trying equally hard to look indifferent. 'Okay, right, if you . . . no, that's no problem. Yeah. Okay. Where? Sure. Fine.' When he put the phone down they were all still staring at him with undisguised anticipation. He shrugged. 'Wants to know if I'll pick her up in the limo tomorrow night. Must be some posh do. Wants me to make sure I'm wearing my chauffeur's uniform.'

Now it was Charisma's turn to be stared at.

He forced a smile. 'It's probably because I told her I wouldn't be seeing much more of her. Well, I like to play the field, y'know.'

They were saved from comment as Tate appeared in the doorway. He looked sick. His voice trembled as he spoke.

'It's gone!'

'What's gone, guv?' Hallam got up, perturbed by the station officer's stricken appearance.

'The money,' said Tate. 'The money we collected for the kid.' Above the babble of disbelief he stumbled on: 'I was going to drop it off at the bank after all, on my way to the hospital to see Cartwright. And it's not there.'

'Guv, you must have looked in the wrong – '

'It's gone, I tell you.' Tate drew a long, shuddering breath. 'Gone.'

3

THE SMELL wafting through the hatch from the kitchen brought Josie Ingham to a halt. Bayleaf saw her stop and sniff, and waited for her to peer in. It suddenly became very important that she should look in and meet his gaze and smile.

Her slender, puckish features were framed in the hatchway. 'If that tastes as good as it smells, I'm going to enjoy today's rations.'

'Thank you, Josephine. I'm glad there's one discerning palate around here.'

'When you've only yourself to cook for,' she said wistfully, 'you tend to settle for a sandwich or a tin of soup.'

He ought not to ask. He ought not to take as much as a slight step in her direction. They both knew that. Yet somehow she was willing him to ask.

'Your old man still on the missing list, is he?'

'Not missing.' She snapped the words out. 'Left. Permanently.'

'Sorry.'

And hadn't he got the right to be sorry for himself, too? Karen had marched out weeks ago, not for the first time, but this time taking everything with her: not just one suitcase of clothes, but her entire wardrobe; and not just their daughter Melanie but all Melanie's clothes and all the pictures from Melanie's room. Later he had discovered she'd taken the family photograph album too. What pleasure could she possibly hope to get out of their wedding photographs and honeymoon photographs and holiday photographs? Oh, he knew all there was to know about an empty flat, and cooking for yourself, and waiting for the hours to trudge by between bed and going on watch again.

He removed a pan from the cooker, nudged the colander into position, and wiped a smear of fat from the edge of the table.

'It occurs to me, Bayleaf,' mused Josie, 'that you could make someone a good wife.'

That was not quite how he wanted her to regard him, but he tried to make a joke of it. 'You know, I did think of asking you over for dinner, showing off some more of my culinary prowess. And it'd make a bit of a change for both of us.' When she looked away, with a faint frowning line across her brow, he said hastily: 'Sorry, bad idea. I wouldn't want you thinking it was some kind of romantic overture. Just a couple of colleagues, you know.'

She looked up again, and a shy gleam of pleasure had crept into her dark, uncalculating eyes. Her uncertain but affectionate smile was worth waiting for. 'In that case,' she said, 'I accept.'

He was so surprised that he found himself stupidly sowing seeds of doubt. 'You sure? I mean – '

'Platonic, right?'

It was all nice and relaxed and easy. 'But I reserve the right' – he was beginning to feel crazily cheerful about what might lie ahead – 'to protect myself against any physical advances.'

'In that case I don't think I'll bother.'

They were both laughing as footsteps came along the passage and the Watch began to line up for their grub. Just one plateful had been dished out when the bells went down.

Hallam was hurrying into the Appliance room with

the print-out, to be greeted with a chorus of disbelief.
'Trapped in a *what*?'

David McBeth had spent many months and a large
amount of money on getting his docklands flat just
the way he wanted it. Light reflected from the river
struck up at the ceiling and then at an angle on to a
row of shimmering abstract paintings along one wall.
His cordless telephone was always placed at a careful
forty-five-degree angle on the Chinese table he had
bought in the King's Road; and the lavender colour of
the phone matched the Thai silk hanging over the long,
low bookcase. He rearranged his books every now and
then to produce a pleasingly irregular pattern according
to the colours and height of the spines rather than author
or subject matter.

His digital watch produced a small chime to warn
him he had five minutes to spare before setting off
for his City appointment. It was followed by another
mellow chime – that of the doorbell.

Impatiently McBeth opened the door without taking
his usual precaution of peering through the Judas
spyhole.

The door crashed back on him. Two men stormed in,
the leader grabbing him by the shoulders and pushing
him violently backwards to collapse on his cherished
chaise-longue. When he tried to struggle up he found
himself looking at the blade of a knife, only a few inches
from his nose.

'Just sit there and no one gets hurt, right?'

One of them was a burly young white man, the other
a tall, spindly black. The black youth had been carrying
a large bag which he dumped with a heavy thud on the
floor. When he straightened up he gazed round the
room, awestruck and delighted.

'Hey, man, can you believe this place?' He prodded

the glass-fronted cupboard in which McBeth had set two pieces of Venetian glass.

'Case you forget, Junior, we're here to rob the geezer,' growled his partner. 'What are you – an estate agent or something?'

'I tell you, Max, just you wait and see. One day soon, this'll be for me.'

The man called Max leered at McBeth. 'It had to happen. Spade yuppies. There goes the neighbourhood.'

Junior turned his attention to a compact disc stack and began fiddling with the knobs.

Max was still hunched above McBeth. 'Right, let's do it. Where's the karzy?'

'The what?' McBeth's voice came out strained and croaky.

'The loo, the toilet, the bathroom, whatever you lot call it.'

McBeth dared to hope that this couple of louts were only amateur thieves, chancers who were already getting frightened in their bowels. He waved towards the door at the end of the room. 'Through there.'

'Okay, right. On your feet. Let's go.'

'I don't understand. I don't want to – '

'On your feet, I said.'

Junior came closer as McBeth tottered upright. He studied the charcoal grey suit with glowing admiration. 'Love the garms, man. Reckon that's my size, or what?'

Max glared. 'Come on.' They hustled McBeth into his bathroom, where Junior marvelled afresh at the puce shower curtain and the marbled bath and lavatory. 'Right, take off your strides and the designer underpants.'

'I want the whole *suit*,' whined Junior. 'He has to take the suit off.'

McBeth could hardly squeeze the words out. 'What are you going to do?'

'Don't worry, mate, we ain't going to hurt you. Just need to make sure we've got plenty of time and no interruptions.'

Max clicked his fingers at Junior, who reluctantly took his eyes off the Paul Smith suit, silk handkerchief and old school tie. He went out, and was back in a moment lugging the bag.

It took only a few more minutes before McBeth found himself naked and forced to stand in the lavatory pan, while cement mix was poured into it and began to set around his ankles. He stood there, listening to their every move as they packed some of his most treasured possessions into his own suitcases, and the click as the music centre connections were pulled from their plugs.

At last the door was slammed behind them. He was left standing there, his feet being squeezed by the setting cement, blood pounding up his legs. It was over an hour before there was any further sound from outside.

'Oh, my Gawd. Whatever . . .'

It was the voice of his cleaner. She must be shuffling across the sitting-room, and he could guess from her moans and squeals just what a shambles the place must have been left in.

He called out and heard her coming towards the bathroom door. 'Oh, you're in there, Mr McBeth. What sort of a mess is this, then?'

'Mrs Whitehouse, I've been robbed. Two men. They threatened me.'

'Two men? Gawd help us. Are you all right?'

He realized too late what a spectacle he would present. 'No, Mrs Whitehouse. Don't come in. Please . . .'

She stood in the doorway, staring. He clapped his hands over his genitals. She seemed incapable of looking away, just standing there and shaking her head, and saying again: 'Are you all right?'

'No, I am *not* all right. I've been robbed, humiliated,

missed an important meeting, and I'm stuck in this bloody toilet. Cemented, d'you understand? For God's sake call the police.'

She withdrew, still dazed. Ten minutes later a young W.P.C. and an even younger P.C. stood there, marvelling just the way Mrs Whitehouse had done; and behind them came a cluster of firemen and one firewoman. Did so many people have to be there, gawping?

The firemen turned off the water and began levering the toilet bowl away from the floor. One of them considerately put his arm around the victim's bare shoulders to steady him; and the mortified McBeth could feel him trembling with suppressed laughter.

There was more laughter when they set the weight of the toilet basin on a small trolley and carted him out into the street to a waiting ambulance, though at least they had been decent enough to cover him in a warm blanket. The collection of ambulance, police car and fire brigade tender had brought half the neighbourhood out. He could hear them burbling and sniggering together as the ambulance set off; and then there was the ordeal at the other end, as doctors and nurses lined up to see him arrive, and patients being wheeled along the corridor brightened up in spite of whatever pain they might have been suffering.

Tate and Hallam heard the commotion from Vaseline's bedside but were too busy with immediate problems to worry about anything else. The questions were made no easier by the presence of Marion Cartwright, holding Vaseline's hand and staring into his eyes and every now and then trying to nuzzle his cheek.

Propped up on his pillows, Vaseline made a big effort to look heroic.

'Listen, Vas . . .' Hallam caught a resentful glance from Vaseline's wife just in time. 'Er . . . Roland. We've

42

been trying to figure out that business of your boots. I mean, catching fire like that.'

'Yes, well, it's one of the hazards, isn't it? No fires, then no jobs for us firefighters.'

Hallam said bluntly: 'Malcolm mentioned something about you using your boots to do a bit of moonlighting. Now, if there was anything that might have – '

'Me?' said Vaseline self-righteously. 'Don't know where Malcolm got that from.'

Marion's eager, sexy little smile went sombre round the edges. 'You might as well tell them.'

'Tell us what?' said Tate bleakly.

Vaseline gave in. 'Well, the thing is, I've been . . . well, using them to do this gardening job I've got.'

'And?'

'Well, I didn't think about it at the time. Thing is, I was using this weed-killer. Only not your normal weed-killer, like, though it does the trick. I mean, I wouldn't personally have . . . only the old bird whose garden it is, she said her husband always insisted – '

'Roland, get to the point.'

'It was sodium chlorate.'

Hallam jolted in his chair as if receiving an injection in his backside. 'Sodium chlorate?'

'Must've spilt it on my boots without realizing.'

'But that bloody stuff is lethal if it's . . . Bleedin' hell, Vaseline.' Tate jerked an apologetic nod in Marion's direction. 'Sorry, but honestly, Roland, didn't you learn about material like that on your basic training?'

'Well, yeah, but . . .' Vaseline shifted uncomfortably in bed. 'It won't . . . uh . . . won't affect my sick pay, will it, guv?'

Hallam did not dare look at the station officer's expression.

Bayleaf had opened out the extra flap to the dining

table, not because it was really needed for two people but because it made more generous space for a vase of flowers in the middle and a wine decanter at the end. The crystal decanter had hardly been used since Karen's uncle had given it to them as a wedding present. He was surprised Karen had not taken it with her. She had always given it pride of place on the sideboard, dusting it every other day and washing it out once a week along with her other meticulous obsessions, but not approving of it being filled with wine. Not that the bottle of wine Bayleaf had bought for this evening was worthy of decanting, so far as he knew; but he fancied making a flourish, to assert something – though he wasn't sure what.

Josie arrived on time, and uneasily he had to admit to himself that he was beginning to be more and more aware of just what it was all about. Even in the station, in uniform and competently, impersonally ready for whatever work came along, she had been getting through to him. Now, here in his own home, off duty, she was taking on a new reality. It was a different Josie now, in her dark green skirt and trim black sweater, the high collar looking almost an extension of her crisp bonnet of short black hair. She would never have dared to wear those dangling hoop earrings at Blackwall.

He took her coat and hung it in the tiny hall. He had no idea what perfume she was wearing, but it was sharp and clean and uncloying – like Josie herself.

She sniffed. A different sort of aroma: his cooking. 'Smells delicious.'

When he had ceremoniously poured her a glass of wine, indicated where she should sit, and then brought the casserole to the table, he said: 'Home cooking – nothing quite like it.'

'Especially if it's done by someone else,' she said appreciatively.

Settled opposite each other across the table, they both ate slowly, neither one willing to start up a conversation that might lead towards anything for which they were not yet ready.

At last Josie spoke. Colleagues, they had agreed. Just mates, talking shop.

'No clues to what happened to that money we collected?'

'Damned shame. Some sneak thief, had to be.'

'The guv'nor doesn't seem too sure about that.' She sipped her glass of wine and smiled seriously across it. 'Says he had it well tucked away at the back of his filing cabinet and nothing else was disturbed or taken. Reckons it has to be someone who knew it was there.'

'Stupid place to leave it, in a filing cabinet. Why not the safe?'

'Red Watch S.O. had rushed out on a shout – with the key in his pocket.'

'There'll be some explaining to do.'

'Yes.' Josie put her knife and fork down and a shadow threatened to fall across the pleasant glow of the evening. 'They'll be asking around, nasty insinuations. Leaning on every one of us.'

'No-one on Blue Watch would nick charity money. Not after all the effort put into it.'

'That's the way I see it, too. And Malcolm's talking of doing another one as soon as we can – an extra push for that kid.'

'Well, I'm game. But I'd still like to know . . .'

The doorbell rang. He looked up at the wall clock. Who the heck could this be at this time of the evening?

He pushed his chair back and went to the front door.

Karen was there, with Melanie holding her hand. It was too glossily obvious that Karen had been to the hairdresser this very afternoon. Her faintly silvery hair had acquired some fashionable streaks, and its always characteristic neatness was now further disciplined into tight little waves and curls.

'Hello,' she said. It was a challenge rather than a greeting.

'What are you doing here?' Bayleaf steadied himself and reached out to stroke his daughter's hair. 'Hello, my girl.' They were staring at him – Melanie imploringly, Karen still with that edge of rancour all too ready to sharpen itself and lash out.

He thought of Josie in the room behind him. There was nothing to do but brave it out.

'You'd better come in.' He led the way through, saying resignedly, 'Josie, this is my wife Karen, and our Melanie.'

Karen stiffened and stopped. 'And who the hell is *she*?' That thin Glasgow whinge of Karen's, which had once seemed so impish and attractive, now grated. It was spiteful and plaintive at the same time, accusing people of something before she was even half-way through a sentence. 'And what is she doing here?'

Josie got up from the table. Bayleaf vainly waved her to stay where she was, but she was managing a brave smile, making it as casual as could be for Karen's benefit.

'Thanks for the eats, Bayleaf.' Her plate was still only half empty. 'We'll have to sort out that charity carve-up in the morning. Nice to have met you, Mrs Wilson.'

She held out her hand. Karen Wilson glared at it. Bayleaf brushed past his wife and daughter, and saw Josie to the door. 'Josie, I'm sorry. I hadn't the foggiest – '

'No, I know the feeling. Gerry's been pretty good at that in the past – rolling up again just when I thought I'd washed him out of my hair.'

46

She smiled a wan smile, quite unlike the easy, outgoing one she had greeted him with at the beginning of the evening. And then she was gone.

Bayleaf closed the door and went back inside apprehensively.

Karen was clearing the table. Having stacked the dishes methodically on the draining board, she came back to the table and moved the vase of flowers an inch to the left. Lifting a couple of the blooms, she pinched the stems and shuffled them all into a more orderly pattern.

Bayleaf said: 'It's great to see you back, love. And don't get any silly ideas about – '

'Melanie, you'd better get off to bed.'

'But Mum, it's too early.'

'Bed.'

Melanie looked imploringly at her father. He said: 'Better do what Mum says, sweetheart. We've got one or two things to talk about.' When he had heard her bedroom door open and close, he said, too jovially: 'Right, where's all the luggage?'

'I've just got that one case for the time being. Just to see.'

'To see what?'

Instead of answering, Karen opened the sideboard drawer and took out a sheet of silver paper. Carefully she cut two squares from it and began lining two ashtrays with them.

Bayleaf watched the familiar, compulsive routine with a sinking heart. Was it all going to be the same all over again?

'Look, love, do you have to – '

'If your fancy piece can't be bothered to keep the place tidy, the least I can do is – '

'She's not my fancy piece. I don't have a fancy piece. Josie Ingham is a mate, like the rest of them. You wouldn't object if I had Malcolm or George Green round, would you? This is the first time I've had Josie here.'

'Screwing here makes a nice change from doing it down at the station, is that it? A bit more private, too, instead of all of you having her on a rota basis in the dormitory between shouts.'

He told himself he was not going to lose his temper. He was not going to give her that satisfaction. 'Karen, there's no need for that kind of talk. Josie's as straight as they come, and a good firefighter as well.'

She was staring him straight in the eyes and yet her gaze was pallid and remote, the way it had become in recent years. She was never quite here. Even though she had decided for some reason and for some unspecified duration to come back home from her mother's, she was still not truly here. 'God,' she said distantly, 'that makes me puke. How nauseatingly fraternal you all pretend to be.'

She went back to tidying up the room, nudging ornaments an inch this way, the fruit bowl two inches that way. He tried to remind himself how he had once loved her so dearly, and that they ought to have another go at loving each other, even if it was only for Melanie's sake. But although she came as a matter of course into their bed that night, she turned over and lay on her side, facing away from him. He knew she was awake half the night, but she did not say a word or make a move. On some impulse she had decided to come home; but there was no telling in which direction her feelings might take her the next morning, or the day after that, or the week after that.

She made his breakfast as usual, though he would have been quite happy for her to stay in bed while he got his own. He kissed her as he left the house, and she accepted it as part of the customary ritual.

48

He went through the Watch as usual, with only two minor shouts, and wondered what on earth to expect when he got home.

Karen and Melanie were out. Perhaps they had gone shopping; or perhaps they had already gone back, yet again, to Karen's mother. He crumpled a couple of paper bags into the waste-paper basket and then stooped to retrieve them. Crazy, absolutely crazy, but he knew that the moment she came in she would pick the stuff out and take it between her fingers to the dustbin at the back of the house. He could not bear to wait and watch her do it. Carrying the basket out, he lifted the lid of the bin and tipped the few fragments in. They fell on a bundle of fabric he half recognized. Disbelieving, he reached in and turned over some of the shreds between his fingers. Some time during the day Karen had gone to the trouble of cutting into neat pieces the jacket he had been wearing when Josie was here.

As he turned back despairingly towards the back door, he saw the kitchen curtain twitch. She was back, her face framed for a moment by the window-pane, with a fixed expression of weird, helpless fanaticism.

4

DUSK WAS making the sordid back street look even
more gloomy and decrepit than it had been in
daylight. The windows of the sweatshop had still not
been cleaned, and the light filtering through them
seemed greasy in itself. Malcolm Cross parked his VW
Golf close to the entrance and watched as Mr Malik's
employees at last left work. Saris swished along the
pavement. Heads turned under silk scarves to gossip,
say goodnight, and make some sad, laughing remark
about tomorrow.

One girl emerged dressed in a trim grey suit, with
no scarf or hat over her gleaming black hair. Malcolm
slid out of the driving seat and waved. She stopped,
peered at him under the pallid streetlamp, and smiled
uncertainly.

He said: 'Good evening. Remember me?'

'I hardly recognized you without your uniform. What
are you doing here?'

'Waiting for you, actually.'

'Oh, yes?'

She was even more glowingly beautiful than he had
remembered. The wretched light enhanced rather than
detracted from the mystery of her deep, dark eyes. Even
the uncertainty of her smile was somehow in tune with
her inner radiance.

'A bit forward and all that, I suppose,' he said apologetically. 'Hope you don't mind, only I remembered
you saying something about working late all this week

and I just thought . . . well, I wondered, actually, whether you'd care for a drink. Or preferably a meal . . . sometime?'

She had a wide, generous mouth. Her almost purple lips were relaxing, the smile becoming less unsure and more welcoming. Still she said nothing.

'Not necessarily tonight,' Malcolm blundered on. He had never before felt so awkward and hamfisted with a girl. But then he had never before met a girl quite like this one. 'But sometime, you know. If you're not actually spoken for, as it were?'

Now she was laughing; but with him, not at him.

'Seems funny.'

'What does?'

'A fireman talking with a posh accent.'

'I'm afraid we're all victims of our conditioning and education.'

'You can say that again.' Her smile faded momentarily, and he was surprised by the fervour in her tone. Then she nodded towards the car. 'Is that yours?'

'Well, yes, actually.'

'You could give me a lift home, if you like.'

He was delighted. Things were working out much more smoothly and agreeably than he had dared hope. He held the passenger door open for her and caught his breath as she slid gracefully past him, the faintest musky scent coming from her throat.

'Where to, then?' She began to give detailed instructions but he interrupted her, glad to be able to boast some specialized knowledge. 'Just the address will do. We firemen are as well trained as taxi drivers when it comes to getting to a destination, and we know all the short cuts.'

He drove slowly, not wanting the interlude to end.

'Of course,' she said, 'this doesn't mean I'm going

to invite you in to meet my parents. My Dad would collapse on his prayer mat.'

'I can imagine.' Stopping at traffic lights, Malcolm stole a glance at her perfect profile. 'Tomorrow evening, then?' he ventured.

'Tomorrow evening,' she said, still looking straight ahead.

'Just one thing.'

'Yes?'

'I don't know your name yet.'

'Samina.'

Samina. It was pure music. That night and on his way to the Station in the morning he found himself absurdly humming it to himself, making a lilting tune and trying to fit some silly, sentimental words to it.

The elation quickly wore off at the end of morning parade.

Station Officer Tate barked the words out. 'In a short while Divisional Officer Thomas will be arriving with a couple of detectives to take your statements about the missing money.'

There was a murmur of resentment. A couple of the men turned to Malcolm, the leading fireman and therefore their spokesman.

He said: 'Excuse me, guv'nor. I sense an infringement of our civil liberties here. As I understand these things, none of us has to give a statement of any kind to the police unless we choose to do so, voluntarily.'

'What's the matter, Malcolm?' growled Sub Officer Hallam. 'You got something to hide?'

'Yeah,' grunted George Green, who had never cared for Malcolm Cross's manner, 'where've you hid the money, Malc?'

'It's the point of principle. Not that one expects a retard like you to comprehend such a concept.'

Sicknote tut-tutted. 'I'd own up if I were you, Malcolm, I really would.'

'All right, all right, turn it in.' Tate looked along the line of the Watch. 'He has a point. None of us has to say anything. But it'd look pretty suspicious, not to say stupid, if we didn't. Right?'

'Right,' said Josie Ingham. Most of the others nodded reluctantly.

'If it's any consolation,' said Tate, 'D.O. Thomas will be present during the – '

'Interrogation,' said Malcolm sourly.

'Interviews, Malcolm, interviews.'

George Green leaned forward to scrutinize his mates along the line. 'I think Charisma ought to have a lawyer present as well.'

'What?' Charisma rose to the bait. 'What's that supposed to mean?'

'Just that you *look* so guilty.'

'Good grief,' moaned Tate.

Grief, indeed. The sort of grief the station could well do without, now or at any time. Tate did not believe any of his men could conceivably have stolen the money. Or the one woman. Whatever their individual failings, he would have sworn he knew each and every one of them too well for that. He had conducted his own enquiry, doggedly spoken to them all even though the whole process turned his stomach, and could still swear to their innocence. Yet who else could have got in? Who else would have had any glimmering of where the money was? None of it made any sense.

The cash ought not to have been put there in the first place. He knew that now, too late; and did not look forward to the questions which would inevitably be levelled at him personally when the inquisitors arrived.

Divisional Officer Thomas was a cheerful man on the surface, very keen on the public image of the Brigade and keen on everyone looking devoted and smiling even in times of crisis. But he was capable of being a martinet when things went wrong and there was nobody around he needed to smile at. Sitting in Tate's office with the sun gleaming through the window on to his bald head, fringed by thick grey sideburns, he established at once that this was one of his days for non-commital grimness; non-committal until he saw exactly which way the wind was blowing.

Detective Sergeant Cooper was a heavily built officer with wide shoulders supporting a wide grey jacket. He had a blunt nose and a thick lower lip which had a habit of sagging in incredulity and then heaving back into place with an implied threat. His sidekick, Detective Constable Pope, showed few signs of being anything other than an admiring audience and occasional loyal copycat.

Cooper tugged at the lower drawer of the steel filing cabinet and peered scornfully into it.

'This was the one?'

'Yes,' Tate admitted.

'You don't keep it locked?'

'What for? This is a fire station, not the Criminal Records Office.'

D.O. Thomas intervened smoothly. 'What S.O. Tate means, sergeant, is that there isn't anything of intrinsic value – '

'Over twelve hundred quid in cash?'

'Nothing,' Thomas insisted, 'normally kept in there.'

'And it's in constant use,' said Tate.

'By everyone in the station, sir?'

'No. Mainly the duty station officer and his sub.'

D.C. Pope was prodding the office door as if expecting it to fall off its hinges. 'Is this normally kept locked?' He was looking for approval from his superior rather than waiting for an answer from the station officer.

'If we get a shout,' said Tate irritably, 'we haven't got time to mess about locking and unlocking doors.'

'Bit of a silly place to put the money though, wasn't it?'

'I suppose I *could* have put it under the floor-boards.'

Cooper and Pope exchanged derisive glances. 'You have a safe,' said Cooper. 'Why didn't you put it in there?'

'The duty guv'nor – Red Watch, it'd be – was out on a shout. He had the key.'

Cooper shrugged meaningfully, though it was impossible to guess exactly what he was thinking. He perched for a moment on the end of Tate's desk, swaying backwards and forwards as if taking the strain of a heavy rope which he would remorselessly wind in before he had finished. After a pause for reflection, or to create a menacing effect, he nodded to Pope to make notes of the precise times involved, and turned his attention to the sub officer.

'How long had you been back off the . . . um, *shout*, isn't that it? . . . before Mr Tate told you he'd discovered the money was missing?'

'About twenty minutes,' said Hallam. 'No, by the time we got cleared away, say thirty, forty minutes.'

'So nobody was on duty here during the shout?'

'No, but . . .' Hallam hesitated, frowning.

'But what?'

'That doesn't mean . . . well, a sneak thief could've . . . I mean, it wouldn't have been too difficult for someone to have entered the station from the yard at the back, say.'

'Possibly. Except,' said Cooper with a sceptical droop

56

of his lower lip, 'this thief knew exactly where to look. Nothing else was disturbed or stolen, was it?'

'Not so far as we've been able to see.'

Cooper brooded for a few moments. Then he announced: 'With your permission, I'd like to get in touch with the station officer on duty at the time, just to verify a few points. Know where I can raise him?'

Tate silently indicated the phone on his desk and the pad of crucial numbers beside it.

'And then,' said Cooper, 'perhaps we can begin interviewing the . . .' He had surely been about to call them suspects. Instead, after another of his calculated pauses, he said: 'The members of the Watch.'

Tate sat back gloomily and waited for the worst. D.O. Thomas was carefully not looking at him, offering no moral support but no outright condemnation; not yet, at any rate.

The first to be wheeled in was George Green. He answered questions sullenly, his face as heavy with latent violence as the detective's. But there was something convincing about his sheer stubborn refusal even to be polite or to try to dodge the questions.

After him came Bayleaf. He looked glum rather than aggressive. Tate felt that Bayleaf's feelings were much on a line with his own. They were both disgusted by the entire proceedings.

Then came Charisma. At the first sight of him, Tate's heart sank.

'Fireman Appleby – that right?'

'Right.' Charisma looked far from right. Always awkward, with apprehensive, puzzled eyes, today he looked downright shifty.

'Perhaps you'll tell us, Fireman Appleby, what it was you were picking up when you called in to the station on the evening of the 24th. You were off duty by then, weren't you?'

57

'I . . . uh . . . what?'

'According to Mr Farmer, the station officer on duty at the time,' said Cooper inexorably, 'he spoke to you at approximately twenty-three hundred hours.'

'Eh? Oh, that.' Charisma was getting more and more flustered. 'Yes, I remember now. I was just collecting something from my locker, actually.'

Tate could not imagine what Charisma was talking about or why he should look so unutterably guilty. But not guilty of stealing the money: Tate would still hold to that. He could only hope he wasn't going to be let down.

He was dying for a drink.

'Personal belongings?' Cooper was pressing Charisma.

'Uh, yes. Yes, that's right.' For some reason Charisma was now looking unhappily at the divisional officer.

Thomas said: 'You don't have to answer these questions if you don't want to, Fireman Appleby.'

'Unless he has something to hide,' contributed Detective Constable Pope.

Cooper glared at him. Tate got the message, and Pope surely must have done. The D. S. was making it plain who was in charge and who would do the questioning.

'Something to . . . uh, no, what would I have to hide?'

'That's what we are trying to establish.' Cooper seemed to be on the verge of licking his thick lips.

'It was nothing. Just my suit.' Again Charisma glanced fearfully at the divisional officer, who for his part looked baffled. Charisma gave a shrug of defeat.' I suppose it was George who told you all about it, eh?'

'George?' said D.O. Thomas.

'Fireman Green. You've spoken to him. He'll have told you.'

Cooper sauntered around behind the hapless Charisma, breathing slow and hard. 'What could Fireman Green tell us?'

'Well, you know. I mean, when he picked me up, like . . . I was with this lady I know . . . knew. He was doing me a favour, as a mate, you know.'

Cooper and Pope exchanged glances. They knew nothing whatsoever, but they were intrigued. So was Tate.

It had clearly begun to dawn on Charisma that his interrogator was in the dark about what had really happened that night. He stalled for time, repeating that he had simply collected his suit because he was taking this girl home, and he had forgotten what he had left in his locker – until it all grew so confused that everyone lost the thread, and Charisma was allowed to go.

One thing Tate was now sure of: when Charisma had spoken of his suit, the detectives had not realized that he meant his fireman's uniform. Tate realized it, but could only hope that the D.O. had not also sussed it. It was against regulations to take uniform off the premises other than for official purposes. Tate would prefer Charisma not to get into trouble with Thomas. He himself was capable of administering enough trouble when necessary.

Josie Ingham was sent for.

Cooper became quite avuncular, but still enjoyed himself, prowling around her and talking to her from behind so that she had to twist her neck to answer him.

He made a brutal beginning. 'I understand your husband has left you.'

'You understand what?'

'That you're separated.'

'What's that got to do with it?'

D.O. Thomas felt it his duty to rally to her support. 'Yes,' he challenged Cooper. 'What *has* it got to do with this, sergeant?'

'People's financial position can often have a bearing on their behaviour, Mr Thomas.'

'My wages are perfectly adequate to cover my "financial position", thank you very much,' Josie burst out.

'Based on past experience, we do have to pursue such lines of enquiry,' said Cooper smugly. 'We've known some sad cases, women left by a husband who's gone off with somebody else. Breadwinner disappears – it can make life very difficult.'

'Breadwinner?' cried Josie, outraged. 'We're not all bloody helpless little females who have to rely on men to support us. I earned more bread than Gerry ever did. He was out of work half the time, always full of big talk and always wanting a handout for . . .' She stopped herself, ashamed of blurting out such revelations. 'It's none of your business.'

Cooper cleared his throat, then found himself caught in the beams of Tate's and Thomas's disapproval. Before he could decide which way to continue, the D.O. said flatly: 'I think your line of questioning is offensive and unproductive. I am advising Firewoman Ingham to give no further answers.'

Cooper tried to look indifferent and dismissed Josie with a wave of the hand. 'Would you mind asking Fireman . . . um . . .' He glanced at Pope, who consulted his list and said eagerly: 'Sanderson.'

'Would you be so kind as to ask Fireman Sanderson if he would care to be next?'

There was an uncomfortable silence between Josie's departure and the arrival of Tony Sanderson.

A patronizing note in Cooper's voice made it clear that

he did not like blacks but would bend over backwards to be tolerant. 'Now, Mr Sanderson. I expect like most of you boys you go in for a bit of moonlighting to supplement your wages?'

Tony sprawled back in his chair, crossing his legs languidly, and allowed himself a grin as patronizing as Cooper's voice.

'I guess that depends on whether you're the police or the tax man.'

Cooper allowed himself a phony smile and turned with equally phony amiability to D.O. Thomas. 'Wish our lot could get away with earning a bit extra on the side.'

'Oh, I dunno, sarge.' Tony slumped further into his chair. 'I do read of the odd case in the court reports.'

'Yes, well.' Cooper was making an effort to keep his voice level and under control. 'Always a bad apple or two in any barrel, isn't there?'

'Yeah, they're the ones that turn black.'

'I don't think Sergeant Cooper was implying anything like that, Fireman Sanderson,' said Thomas uncomfortably.

'Like what, sir?' Tony was all innocence.

'You know. Prejudice.'

'I'm sure you're right, sir.'

D.O. Thomas wasn't the only one who was feeling uncomfortable. Tate shifted in his chair. What the hell had got into Tony? He was rarely as prickly as this about his colour. There was something wrong. He had come in here all hyped up to be defensive and aggressive at the same time. The whole atmosphere made Tate uneasy.

'Right,' said Cooper. 'Uh . . . where were we?'

'Moonlighting,' said Tony.

'Well, no matter. Accepted practice, nobody gets

hurt. And who doesn't have bills to pay?' He tried a heavy-handed joke with the D.O. 'And I don't mean Ol' Bills.'

Thomas managed the obligatory smile. Tony went on staring straight ahead, ready to snap back at whatever was thrown at him.

Bayleaf had just finished cleaning out the appliance when Josie came round the rear of the turntable. She smiled nervously and was about to quicken her pace when he said:

'Jose, I haven't had a chance to talk to you since the other evening.'

'That's okay.' She kept her distance. 'I understand.'

She looked so vulnerable. He wanted to reach out and touch her. But not here; and not with her as taut as she was right at this moment.

'I want to apologize for that bit of embarrassment,' he went on. 'You know, my missus turning up out of the blue like that.'

'I had nothing to feel embarrassed about. It was your wife that got upset.'

'I suppose it did look a bit sus from her point of view, you know.'

'Two colleagues just having dinner?'

'Yes, well, you know.'

'Sure,' said Josie wryly, 'I know.'

There was the echoing clump of boots across the Appliance room. Sub Officer Hallam, with a sheaf of papers in his hand, looked questioningly at Josie. She returned his gaze stonily and went on her way.

'Not interrupting anything, am I?' he asked.

'No,' said Bayleaf. 'And what's that supposed to mean?'

Hallam made sure that Josie had before he spoke.

'Just that your missus called round to "visit" mine. And guess who she was asking questions about?'

Bayleaf thought of Karen sitting across the teacups from Sandra Hallam and whining out her miseries and spiteful fantasies. She maliciously calculated that Sandra was bound to pass the gossip on to John Hallam, who would be bound to drop some hints to the rest of the Watch. He was about to come out with a complaint of his own when Hallam moved away, glancing back for no more than a moment.

'Word to the wise, that's all.'

Bayleaf finished off, went for a wash, and made his way slowly towards the mess. Josie was approaching from the opposite direction. She tried to get to the door before him as if to avoid any further awkward conversation, but he said: 'Jose, there's something you ought to know.'

She stopped reluctantly. 'What's that?'

'Karen called round to see Hallam's missus. Seems she was asking about us.'

'That figures. She's probably doing the rounds.'

'I'm sorry. Wouldn't have occurred to me.'

'Then you've still got a lot to learn about women, haven't you?'

He followed her into the mess. Heads turned, then everybody pretended to be immersed in eating or reading the sporting pages of the paper. You could sense that the talk had already got this far.

Loudly, to cover up the giveaway silence, Malcolm said: 'By the way, George, how did you make out with Charisma's ex? We're all dying to know.'

George had been surreptitiously grinning to himself. Now the grin was wiped off his face. 'What? Oh, yeah. Her.'

'Well?'

'Okay, I guess.'

'Okay? Is that all you're going to reveal?'

Charisma glanced covertly along the table.

'Tell you the truth,' said George, 'she was a bit weird.'

'She'd have to be' – Tony did not even look up from his paper – 'to go out with you and Charisma.'

'"Curiouser and curiouser!"' Malcolm was not going to relent. 'Come on, old chap, I want to hear every sordid detail.'

'You would, wouldn't you,' said Josie contemptuously on her way to the serving hatch.

'Ah, Firewoman Ingham. And how, dare one ask, is *your* love life?'

'Much the same as yours, I'd imagine – restricted to the odd wet dream.'

They all became aware of two figures standing in the doorway. The two detectives, less aggressive than they had been up till now, were looking at the plates and then at the serving hatch, but were unsure of their welcome.

Bayleaf waved them in. 'Find a seat at the trough.'

Tony and George shifted to either side to make room; plenty of it. Cooper and Pope had just settled themselves when the bells went down. They gaped at the speed of the response as Josie and the men leaped up and dashed for the door. It was of course purely accidental that a teapot and a jug of milk should be knocked into Pope's lap.

'Sorry, mate,' George Green called from the door. 'You'll probably find seconds in the kitchen.'

The old woman had taken a last look at the photograph of her late husband on the mantelpiece, and then laid out his best suit on the bed beside her wedding gown, yellowing now but still immaculate in its swathes of tissue paper. She climbed painfully up the steps from the basement flat, and went to stand at the busy corner. Streetlights cast orange splashes across the rain-soaked road. Headlights came dazzlingly at her and flashed past. She waited until the oncoming lights were those of a large lorry, its tyres hissing over the wet surface, and then threw herself forward.

Brakes screeched. The lorry swerved, bumped hideously over flesh and bone, and slewed right across the road into the path of a small van. The van was struck so hard that its back doors flew open. A car ploughed between them and jolted to a halt. Another car was heading the same way. The young mother driving it turned her head just once, for a few seconds, to tell the children in the back seat to stop squabbling. It was a few seconds too many. When she turned back to face the road it was to see piled-up vehicles immediately in front of her. She screamed. Brakes screeched again. A wisp of flame began to lick from the bonnet of the van.

The howl of approaching fire engines cleared the streets, but it was difficult to manoeuvre them close to the tangle of metal and trapped bodies. A child was squealing hysterically. The lorry driver had freed himself from his cab but was leaning against the front wheel, gasping for breath, incapable of any further movement.

The firemen rolled out the hoses to deal with the van. Sicknote and Malcolm Cross fought a way to the twisted wreckage of the car, bracing themselves against a buckled door and beginning to cut through panels until they could lift a whole section out. They sawed, lifted, heaved. Josie and George Green moved in behind them, lifting the unconscious woman with infinite care from a seat covered in blood. One of the kids went on screaming. The other was limp but alive, beginning to mumble and sob. 'All right, love, we've got you.' Blankets were wrapped around them. 'Your Mum's all right. Don't worry.' The ambulance was edging into position. George carried the little girl tenderly in his arms, stepping carefully over hoses and torn shreds of metal. Tate's white helmet cruised between yellow helmets like a shark's fin through the waves of chaos.

Bayleaf, covering the crushed remains of the old woman with a tarpaulin, said: 'Her head's missing.'

Malcolm, stepping back, gagged but braced himself. Then Sicknote, stooping to free a hose, sagged against the side of the crumpled car and threw up all down it.

'Good God.' Hallam was picking his way towards them. 'First time I've seen him genuinely ill. What is it?'

Bayleaf peered under the car. 'Oh, shit. It's that old lady's head.'

By the time they had finished, Red Watch would have taken over for night duty at the station. Blue Watch were silent on the way back, totally exhausted. Tate kept a careful eye on Sicknote, afraid he might throw up again and they would have to clean the appliance even more carefully than usual.

Tony and George Green helped Sicknote down and steered him towards the washroom.

'Never mind, Sicknote,' Malcolm called after them. 'Remember the old saying, "If you can keep your head when all around you lose theirs . . ."'

'Leave it out,' snapped Hallam. He looked round at the rest of them. 'Anyone fancy a drink?'

'I'd better get home.' Bayleaf was staring accusingly at Hallam as he spoke. 'Just to report that I'm . . . safe, right?'

Josie wiped one hand down her smeared face, and said something about washing her hair.

Malcolm said: 'I'm meeting a friend. And it looks like I'm going to be late.'

★   ★   ★

The lights were subdued and the restaurant was dry and warm, all very different from the harsh lights and swirling rain and filthy street corner he had left so recently. Malcolm looked across the table at Samina, and waited for the tension to leave his bones and muscles.

When the waiter had moved away, she said: 'Do you bring all your dates here?'

'Not all of them.'

She was smiling. He felt himself smiling, too – unable to stop. Now they had all the time in the world.

'Tell me more about you and India,' she said. 'I'd really like to know a bit more – a lot more – about you.' She was so calm, so graceful, and sweetly attentive.

'My parents were caught up in the tail end of the Raj. They debated whether to come home, as they called England. Inexplicable, really, when you consider they'd spent the greater part of their lives in India.'

'And did they come "home"?'

'In the end, no.'

'They stayed with the culture they knew,' she said softly, 'but would never become a part of.'

Half-way through the first course he felt there was something he had to say. 'Samina, that place you work in . . .'

'What about it?'

'Do you have to? I mean, you're so bright and attractive and obviously too intelligent to go on slaving away at a routine job like that.'

She looked gravely into his eyes. 'You've met the boss, Malik. Well, believe it or not, he's a relative. A distant one, but a relative. He played a big part in arranging my parents' marriage, and he paid Mum's expenses to come over to this country. Me working for him is my Dad's way of repaying him.'

'But that's terrible, in this day and age – '

'It's the way things are,' she said levelly. 'My Dad doesn't think women, whether they be wives or daughters, should be encouraged to make decisions about their own lives.' Before Malcolm could protest, she went on: 'It's not his fault. I love him and I try to respect him. Like you said, we're all victims of conditioning.'

'Is he aware of the conditions you work in?'

Her smile came back, with a touch of sadness. 'By the standards he's used to, they're quite acceptable.'

Malcolm said bluntly: 'We're applying for a prohibition order to get the place closed down, you know.'

'Then I'll be out of a job. I'm not worried about myself too much, but most of the women there really do need the work.'

'He'll be able to operate again once he complies with the fire regulations. It's not bureaucracy, you know. It's genuine concern about people's safety and welfare.'

She nodded. Then, eager to change the subject, she nodded again, this time at the scallop shell of seafood on her plate. 'This is very nice.' She glanced around the restaurant. 'You know, I'm not used to all this.'

'I'll let you into a little secret,' said Malcolm. 'On what I earn, neither am I.'

5

THE PUB was noisy and brassy. Dorothy Sanderson usually enjoyed going into pubs with her friend Penny, or with Tony – except when drinkers nudged one another and muttered remarks about black man's meat – but she hated this place the moment she set foot inside the door. Only desperation kept her moving forward. She had dumped so much stuff from the flat for a miserable few quid. Now came the difficult part.

Two young blokes by the beer pumps eyed her up and down and looked hopeful. She swerved away and leaned over the far end of the bar, earning herself a suspicious look from the barmaid.

'Excuse me. Can you tell me if there's a Mr Payne in at the moment?'

The girl raised her skimpy plucked eyebrows and jerked a thumb towards a man standing in the middle of a group of cronies, all of them obviously buttering him up.

Dorothy wanted to turn and run away, but she had to go through with this. Nervously she approached him.

'Are you . . . er . . . Mr Payne?'

He had a shiny grey suit and a shiny greasy complexion. He exuded an easygoing friendliness but there was something sour and calculating in his eyes. It was as if he already knew what Dorothy was here for. His arm went in an unconvincingly friendly hug round her shoulders and he guided her away from the bar.

'Can I help you, darling?'

'You *are* Mr Payne?'

'Nobody else but. And what can I do for you?'

Dorothy felt her throat seizing up. She tried to clear it, and said croakily: 'My friend told me you lend money.'

'Who's your friend?'

'Mrs Rush. Eileen. We live in the same block of flats. York House.'

He ushered her to a table and smiled at her. She thought he was going to offer her a drink; but he was the kind of man who brought drinks for his mates, not for women needing his help.

'And how much did you have in mind?'

'I . . . there's these debts . . . and settling up a few things and . . .' Now she was here, she hadn't the foggiest idea how much was needed to clear it all. 'Say eight hundred?' she hazarded.

'Sure. By all means let's say eight hundred.' Payne looked round. 'But not here. Come into the snug.'

There was a small bar opening off to one side, an old-fashioned relic preserved in the middle of the tarted-up bars and the winking, burbling fruit machines. Dorothy was not happy about being in there alone with this man, whose eyes widened and narrowed in an eccentric rhythm which bore no relation to anything he was actually saying. But he was not interested in her as a woman – only as a business proposition.

She watched as he dug out a roll of notes from his back pocket. They flicked out on to the little round table between them: five, six, seven . . . eight hundred.

Payne said: 'Your old man know you're borrowing this?' When she shook her head, he grinned with a flash of two gold teeth. 'Yeah, that's usually the way.' He kept his hand on the money for a moment. 'So how are you going to make the payments?'

'I'll get a job.'

He studied her for a moment, sizing her up as if trying to assess her potential as a streetwalker or stripper. 'Okay,' he conceded. 'Providing you pay up regularly it'll be our little secret. 'Course, if you don't, I'll be obliged to have a word in his ear. And we wouldn't want any domestic strife, would we?' When Dorothy could think of no reply, he went on with oily satisfaction: 'Right, darling. Now let me explain to you my modest interest rates, plus methods of payment . . .'

She went back home feeling both relieved and terrified. It was all very well to talk of getting a job and paying him off, but at least the immediate problem of the debts and demands and dunning letters had been averted. Tony ought to be pleased with her. Only she wasn't going to tell him what she had lumbered herself with. It would all work out, it had to. She was determined to make it work out.

By the time Tony came in, her self-assurance was ebbing. The weight of paying off this new debt was looming larger than the thought of Tony's face when he saw the money and knew their troubles were over.

'You in, love?' he called from the hall. She heard him moving, light-footed and loping as ever, into the living-room. There was a long pause before he headed for the kitchen.

'Hello, love.' She got up and flung her arms round him. His body was warm against hers; always so warm, was Tony.

'Where's all that stuff gone?' he demanded. 'The stuff from the front room?' And when she pointed triumphantly to the scattering of notes on the formica top of the kitchen table he said incredulously: 'And where d'you get *that* from?'

'I sold a lot of those things I bought.' She had rehearsed this several times over before he got back, and was gabbling it out. 'Things we didn't need, like you said. So we could pay off the bills, you know.'

He looked stunned. 'Second-hand? You sold it all off second-hand?'

'Well, yes. I mean, how else could I – '

'For crying out loud, Dorothy. How the hell are you going to pay off the bills on goods you paid the full price for, with the price you get for them second-hand? That doesn't add up. Are you crazy?' He stared at the money. 'How much you got there?'

No matter what problems she had laid up for herself later, she had expected him to be pleased right now. She couldn't bear that critical expression of his, not again. 'Enough to pay off all the credit card bills. Over a thousand, all told.'

'You got over a thousand for a load of old used goods?' He shook his head, dazed. 'That's not possible. Who give you that kinda money for that kinda crap?'

It was all going wrong, when all she had wanted to do was to put everything right. 'It's not all of it from selling off stuff. I'm going to get a job. Made some enquiries. Got a sort of advance. I thought if we had a bit of extra weekly money . . . I mean, I got two hundred and seventy for the stuff I sold.' She opened her handbag and added the notes to the pile. 'So that's a good bit towards it. I wasn't going to tell you, but – '

'Dorothy. Stop this.'

'But Tony, I thought you'd be pleased. I thought it'd give us a fresh start, it – '

'What ain't you telling me?'

She wanted to hold out, but she always shrank when he looked at her like that. 'I borrowed the rest,' she whispered.

He was flabbergasted. 'Lemme see if I've got this. You borrowed actual cash money?'

'Well, it's more a sort of H.P., you know.'

'How much?'

She felt tears choking into her throat. 'Don't get upset, Tone, please.'

He slammed his fist down on the table. A couple of notes floated to the floor. '*How much*?'

'Eight hundred quid.' For an instant she thought he was going to hit her. Instead, his face crumpled in defeat and he slumped down into the chair opposite.

'It's not as bad as it seems,' she pleaded. 'At least it's easier to pay off the debt in instalments instead of having threatening solicitors' letters and all that. I don't want to go to court. I couldn't do it.'

His hand was over his eyes. 'Who lent you eight hundred pounds, honey?'

'This bloke. You know Eileen, two doors along? She told me about him.'

Tony lowered his hand and stared at her. 'His name doesn't happen to be Sharky Payne by any chance?'

'You know him?'

'Everybody round here knows about that skunk,' said Tony dully, 'except you.'

He stood up and reached for the money. He was on his way towards the front door before she could say: 'Tony? Tone, what are you going to do?'

He did not look back.

Sharky Payne was at the bar drinking with two of his hangers-on. They were tougher looking than Payne. When you got as flabby as Sharky Payne, you needed two hard men in the near vicinity to deal with any awkwardness.

Tony Sanderson crossed the floor and flung the eight hundred pounds on to the bar. 'That's from my wife, Mrs Sanderson. She don't need no loan from you, right?' He turned to leave.

Payne made a grab for his shoulder. 'Hold it, black boy.'

'Boy?' echoed Tony softly. 'Guess that makes you my dog.'

Sharky glanced at the money and allowed himself a menacing smile. 'How much is there?'

'Eight hundred. That's what you lent her, that's what you get back.'

'I ask for interest on money I lend. That's the business I'm in.'

'Interest? You're joking. She ain't had it a day.'

'In particular I ask for high interest on short-term loans. The shorter the term, the higher the interest. Matter of fact, as a businessman I *demand* it.'

'You're a loan shark,' said Tony with deadly composure. 'That makes you a thief, and you ain't stealing from my wife.'

'I wouldn't be. I'd be taking it from a nigger's whore.'

Tony's right fist came up in a long, swinging arc. It jabbed into Sharky's left jaw and threw him back against the corner pillar of the bar. His two heavies shoved themselves forward, ready for action.

'I wouldn't do that, man.' The bar was suddenly crowded with six of Tony's friends, two of them holding baseball bats, one an iron tyre-lever. 'Not unless,' said Claude, the leader, with some relish, 'you want your faces to look like your arseholes.'

Tony was walking with some spring in his stride as he approached home. He took the steps two at a time on the way to the third floor balcony. Only at the scratched blue door did he stop, with the weight of uncertainty coming back to douse his exuberance. It was all very well to put on a big moral act and get rid of that money. There was a small matter of some other money which, like Dorothy's efforts, would cover those bills. Now he knew with a sinking heart that it couldn't be used.

Dorothy was waiting for him on the edge of the settee with a damp handkerchief crumpled into her right palm. She hardly dared look into his face. He sat down beside her and put his arm around her. Thankfully she collapsed against his shoulder.

'You shouldn't have done it, precious.' He kissed her. 'But thanks.'

'I had to ring Claude. He said they'd probably beat you up. I was scared.'

'So was I, but that's not what I'm talking about. I meant the money. Root of all evil, eh?' He took a deep breath. He had to get this out of his system here and now. 'And there's something else. Dorothy, there's something I got to tell you right here and now. And it's not gonna make you very proud of me.'

Josie Ingham crossed the Appliance room past Bayleaf, rolling a hose and reached in to collect the log-book. Quietly, without raising his head, he said: 'She's gone again.'

'What d'you mean, gone? Away? Peculiar, or what?'

'Gone away. Left and taken Melanie. That poor kid don't know what the hell's going on.' He flicked the end of the hose and caught Charisma's ankle as he came unexpectedly round the front of the vehicle. 'Sorry, Charisma, didn't see you there.'

'No one ever does.' It was Hallam, sauntering out of the Watch room.

'Ever does what?' asked Josie.

'Notice Charisma.'

'I do.' She found Hallam's derisive tone so offensive she had to spring to the defence of a mate.

'Oh? Didn't think he was your type.'

'Perhaps you should ask your wife.'

Hallam blinked. 'Pardon?'

'And while you're at it, sub, you might tell her that if my private life is of such interest then she and the other wives ought to invite me to one of their silly little tea parties.' She folded her arms and out-stared him. 'I can discuss the juicier bits with them. Tell them how I spend my duty hours undressed in a dormitory with their husbands. All those little private things, you know?'

She left him speechless and was glad when she could go home and put the whole place behind her for another day.

Only it did not work out quite like that. As she was crossing the road, Dorothy Sanderson came trotting along to catch her up. 'Josie, please, I've got to talk to you.' She glanced apprehensively back towards the station. 'If we could just get out of the way a bit.'

They turned down a side street towards the little patch of public park with its muddy pond and despondent elderly men who littered the seats with empty cider bottles and crumpled newspapers.

'Something wrong?' Josie prompted, when Dorothy seemed incapable of saying what she had come here to say.

'He'd go barmy if he knew I'd told you, but I've just got to speak to someone from the station who'll . . . well, understand . . . just in case they . . .'

'Dorothy.' Josie came to a halt. 'Whatever it is, could I have it in words of one syllable, in the right order?'

Dorothy stared out over the pond and talked breathlessly. 'The money. That charity money. It was Tony who took it. And hid it. And it's all my fault.'

'Your fault?'

'Buying things. Things we couldn't afford. And things we didn't even need. I don't know what it was. It was like some sort of aberration – you know,

76

a sort of obsession. And he got panicky over the cost of everything, and took that money we'd collected and hid it away. And now he wants to put it back and doesn't know how. And it's all my fault,' Dorothy wailed again.

Josie put a hand on her arm. 'Take it easy. It'll be all right. Somehow it'll be all right.'

'You won't tell anyone? You're not going to let Tony know I've told you?'

'I won't breathe a word, I swear.'

'It's not fair. I couldn't help myself, and Tony, he's so . . . well, so . . .'

'Honest?'

'Yes. Honest.' Dorothy snuffled a tearful laugh. 'I suppose that sounds silly, considering.'

'No, it doesn't.'

'Because he didn't really take it, you know. It's still there, hidden in the station store-room. He couldn't go through with it. And now he doesn't know what to do.'

They took two turns round the pond while Josie brooded. No point in her offering to collect the money and leave it around where someone could find it, just as if it had been dropped. Tony Sanderson would want to know how it had happened; would live in fear for months, wondering who had known and why the money had been shifted that way. It had to be Tony himself who put it back.

Josie said: 'Look, Dorothy, why don't you get Tony primed for tomorrow. When there's some sort of diversion – out in the yard'd be best, when we're on maintenance – he's to get into the store-room, get that money out, and whizz it along to Tate's office where it was originally.'

'But suppose there isn't any diversion?'

'I'll make sure there is.' Josie grinned. 'Tell you what,

without making it too obvious maybe I could ask him to get me something from the store. It'll be up to him then. I'll have to play it by ear, and so will Tony.'

'But if I tell him we've set it up, he'll know I've talked to you.'

'You don't tell him. All you tell him is that he's to grab any opportunity that presents itself. And I'll find some way of presenting it without him recognizing me as Santa Claus.'

Dorothy dabbed at her eyes. She was a creature of ups and downs. Within a few seconds she was on top of the world again. Somehow the decision had been taken out of her hands and she was free to think of enjoying herself again. She confided that she had been so miserable lately that she had hardly dared to go out. But now she decided to accept her neighbour Jennifer's invitation to go out with some friends as she used to, all girls together. Just a few drinks, a bite to eat, a wander round the neighbourhood laughing and telling silly jokes.

Only as they were parting did a shadow fall momentarily over Dorothy again.

'You won't let Tony guess – '

'I won't let him guess a thing,' said Josie patiently.

Hallam came out of the Watch room as the pump ladder slowed down and swung into the yard. 'How'd it go, then?'

'All right,' Tate grunted.

'All right?' Josie's eyebrows went up. 'Some dear old lady has to barricade herself into her bedroom because her daughter and her cretinous old man want to shovel her off to some O.A.P. prison.' She turned to Bayleaf. 'It was diabolical, right?'

For some reason he was unresponsive, just shrugging and looking away.

She could see Tony Sanderson drifting away from the

group. Josie raised her voice, starting to harangue Tate and Hallam and keep them here as Tony disappeared into the building. 'I mean, I ask you. Selfish slags. People like that make me sick. I mean he actually said, "She's old," like it was leprosy or something.'

'Yeah, well, maybe he had a point,' growled Hallam.

'A point? She was lovely. You should've seen the stuff she'd stacked against the door.' Again she appealed to Bayleaf. 'Right?'

For some reason he appeared to be trying to eyeball her a warning.

'And what makes *you* such a bloody expert?' Hallam positively spat the words out as he strode back into the Watch room.

Josie watched him, open-mouthed. 'What was all that about?'

'I tried to give you the nod,' said Bayleaf.

'About what?'

Tate said: 'His father-in-law's just moved into his house to live. Permanently. It's beginning to drive him up the wall.' He headed inside.

'Oh, Lor'.' Josie saw Tony sauntering along beside the wall and round the side of the pump ladder. 'Trust me and my big mouth, eh?'

Bayleaf looked fleetingly at her mouth, and then looked away.

They set about readying the appliance for its next call. They had been at it about ten minutes when Tate reappeared, brandishing a bulging buff envelope.

'It's back!' he exclaimed incredulously. 'Our charity collection.'

Hallam put his head out of the Watch room. 'All of it?'

'Every penny. Back in the filing cabinet like it's never been away.'

'We couldn't have overlooked – '

79

'No, we couldn't. It was definitely there, and then it was definitely not there. And now it *is* there again.'

'Makes no sense.' As the rest of them gathered joyfully around, Hallam added: 'What are you going to do?'

'Have to let friend Cooper know. And the D.O. They'll probably say just what you did.' Tate looked lovingly at the envelope. 'But since we never did get a hint of who took it, we'd have one hell of a job establishing who put it back. And frankly I don't want to get involved with that. I'm just bloody relieved they did.'

'So now,' said Tony Sanderson smoothly, 'we can have that piss-up and presentation after all.'

'A bit late,' said Tate, 'but yes, we can have it all right.'

6

JOHN HALLAM looked down from the bedroom window on to the back lawn. He was trying to get ready to go on watch and at the same time work out what on earth his father-in-law was doing in the far corner of the garden. Old Albert simply could not keep his hands to himself. He scattered the morning paper into several different pieces all over the living-room, fiddled with salt and sugar canisters in the kitchen and made a cocktail of both on the worktop; and was now groggily down on his hands and knees poking at various plants.

Smitten with alarm, Hallam opened the window.

Sandra came down the path beside the house. 'Good God, Dad, what do you think you're doing?'

'Doing? What's it look like I'm doing, girl?' Albert wheezed. 'I'm pulling up the weeds.'

'They're not weeds,' Sandra exploded. 'They're John's *Viola wittrockiana*. He's only just put them in.'

Her father's bleary eyes turned derisively up towards her. He shook his head in a slow, knowing dither. 'Get out of it! Them's weeds. I know a weed when I see one.'

'Oh, God.' Sandra glanced fearfully over her shoulder. 'He's going to go mad. You know what he's like about his garden.'

Albert's head wobbled as he glanced around the flowerbeds, and he rubbed a drip at the end of his nose. 'If you ask me, he's a bleedin' poofter.'

Hallam slammed the window shut and pounded down

the stairs. He had only ten minutes to spare, but he was not going to let the old sod get away with this.

'What the hell have you been doing to my plants?'

Albert sniggered and looked slyly away.

'Don't do your nut,' Sandra begged. 'He thought they were weeds. I mean, they do look a bit like weeds at that stage, don't they?'

Hallam stood looking down at his father-in-law. He would dearly have loved to lock his hands round his neck and squeeze hard. 'From now on,' he said, 'you're barred from the garden. Understood? This garden is now out of bounds to marauding, senile old – '

'John!'

Hallam stormed on. 'You've pulled up my *Viola wittrockiana* – '

'Load of rubbish. What kind of name is that for – '

'They're pansies. My pansies.'

'Yeah, and I'll bet you know a lot of them too, don't you?' Albert cackled. 'Why don't you get an allotment and grow vegetables like a proper bloke?'

Hallam could hardly believe his ears. This messy old wreck could surely not be hinting . . . He looked at Sandra who could say nothing, caught between the two of them.

Hallam stamped out and got into his car.

He was in no better mood when he went into the mess for a cup of tea. There was a lot of noise going on. Vaseline was back from hospital, revelling in a rowdy welcome and rattling on with a lot of comments about beautiful nurses. He grinned complacently. There had, he admitted, been one or two pleasant interludes. Marion, though, had not been best pleased to come visiting one day and find him in the middle of being given a blanket bath, all too clearly exhibiting his response to the nurse's warm, stimulating hands. It was just as well that he was out and about again.

He ambled towards the serving hatch and shoved his head through the opening. 'But now I *am* out, that makes me available again round here, eh Maggie?'

'Get off with you.' She was a chirpy Cockney, with hair permed in a style too youthful for her age and plumpness, but without too many illusions about herself or anyone else on the station.

'Anyway,' said Vaseline ingratiatingly, 'it'll be good to taste some real grub after the reprocessed corpses I've been used to.'

'Don't get too excited. Me holidays is due soon.'

'Where you going this time?'

'Moscow.'

There was a roar of comment. Hallam grimly seized the nearest newspaper and buried himself in it. Too much more of this fat-headed babble and he would blow his top.

'It'll make a change,' contributed Vaseline. 'Because you don't do no *Russian* to serve us around here, eh?'

There was a mutual groan.

'It's havin' to suffer you lot,' said Maggie, 'that's made me decide to defect.'

Hallam glared over the top of his paper at Josie and Bayleaf, sitting side by side at the table. His lip curled. Before he could start pretending to read again, Charisma said airily into the middle of nowhere: 'Anyone know any good father-in-law jokes?'

They were interrupted by the clangour as the bells went down, and Hallam escaped to the Watch room to pick up details. Some unfortunates, it appeared, had got themselves stuck in a lift.

There were three of them. The two women who lived in the high rise block were all too used to the lift breaking down. But they were not used to having to share the delay with each other; nor with the nervous man who found himself in this situation, very much wishing he had never set eyes on the blonde Sue. With her leather mini-skirt, red leather jacket swinging loose, skimpy red blouse making it clear that she wasn't wearing a bra, and tarty make-up applied in thick swathes, she made a lurid picture alongside the middle-aged Mrs O'Gorman with her drab coat and knitted blue bonnet. Sue gushed and wriggled. Mrs O'Gorman was sour and would undoubtedly have described herself as respectable; the sort of word she would set great store by. It was obvious that she would never in a month of Sundays have applied such a word to her neighbour.

The two women had had their claws out within a few seconds of arriving at the ground floor entrance to the lift.

Sue had squeezed Alan Worsley's arm as she noticed his critical look at the shabbiness of the building and the graffiti sprayed on the concrete columns. 'I'm moving out soon. Asked the council for a swap.'

'Not before time,' muttered Mrs O'Gorman.

Worsley stood back to let her into the lift. She nodded curtly but could not summon up a smile. She pressed her back against the side of the lift as Sue flounced in, as if to avoid any risk of contamination, and glared accusingly at Worsley.

They had just passed the fifth floor when the lift jarred, shuddered once, and stopped. Worsley leaned across Sue to press a button. She rubbed herself against his arm; but that was the only movement.

He mopped his brow. If there was one thing he hated, it was confined spaces. And the smell in here was already making him feel faintly sick.

'Don't worry,' said Sue brightly. 'It's always breaking down.'

'But how do we attract attention?'

'Someone'll notice, and then they'll get the fire brigade. We're used to it.'

She leaned against him and tickled his chin. Any enthusiasm he had felt before was gone by now. He didn't want to go up to her flat; wouldn't have been capable of what had seemed so desirable twenty minutes ago; simply wanted the lift to descend and let him out so that he could go back to dullness and safety.

Mrs O'Gorman eyed them and sniffed. 'Fine to-do, I must say. This used to be a respectable block of flats.'

'Why don't you mind your own business, you nosey old crab.'

'Don't you call me a crab, you . . . you tart.'

'Well, your husband's certainly got that notion,' said Sue, 'the number of times he's tried to grope me in here and on the landing.'

You could almost taste the hatred in the stifling air. Worsley threw himself at the door and began hammering on it with his fists.

'It's no use making all that noise,' said Mrs O'Gorman contemptuously. 'It won't get them here any quicker.'

'How do we know anyone's even got round to reporting it?'

'They will,' said Sue.

'Someone always does,' said Mrs O'Gorman.

'Yeah, there's always someone in these flats who reports *everything*.' The heat between the two women was intensifying.

It seemed an age before there was a faint howling in the distance, and muffled noises from somewhere below. A man was shouting something. They could see nothing, nor hear anything clearly; they could only guess.

The shouts came from an elderly man leaning over

the third-floor balcony as the pump arrived and Hallam sprang down. 'About bloody time.'

'You that raised the alarm, was it, sir?'

'Bloody right. Got an invalid wife up here, ain't I? Wheelchair case she is, isn't she? How am I supposed to get her up and down these stairs with no lift working, eh? Eh? You tell me that.'

'Do you know which floor it's stuck on?'

'How the bloody hell should I know? That's the third time this month. Sick of it, I am, sick of it. *And* you lot with your hooters blaring.'

The man disappeared back into his flat.

'Ignorant old sod,' Hallam muttered.

'Remind you of someone, does he, sub?'

Hallam gritted his teeth and led the way indoors. He unlocked the outer door of the lift shaft with his master key and peered up to the top. It looked as if the lift had jammed between the fifth and sixth floors.

'Right, Appleby and Medhurst – the motor room.'

Charisma groaned. 'I had to climb all the way up on the last one. Why me?'

Half-way up the stairs it might dawn on him that his crack about the sub's father-in-law could have had something to do with that selection.

Hallam beckoned to Vaseline and trudged up the steps to the fifth floor. The other two went plodding on towards the top. Again Hallam used his key to open an outer door, to find the lower eighteen inches of the lift's inner door just above their heads. He reached out and banged on it.

'Anyone in there?'

'Thank God, they're here,' babbled a man's voice. There was an answering bang on the door. 'Hello, hello.'

'All right, sir,' said Hallam soothingly. 'It's the fire brigade. How many of you in there?'

'Three of us. Three.'

'Yeah,' said a young woman's voice, harsh and derisive, 'two's company, three's definitely a crowd.'

'Tart!'

'Crab!'

Vaseline beamed at Hallam. It all sounded fascinating.

'If you could just get us out of here, please, as quickly as possible. I don't actually feel very well.'

Hallam bent over his radio. 'Appleby, you up there yet?'

'Hang on, sub.' Charisma's breathlessness rasped into the receiver. 'Only just got here. A bit dark. Someone's bashed in the light bulb. Kev . . . the torch . . . get the power switch.' There was a pause, then: 'Right, sub. Power's off.'

'Right. When you've released the brake shoes it needs to come *down*.'

'Can't see a bloody thing up here.'

'God, what's keeping them?' the man in the lift was wailing.

'The tax-payer,' said Sue.

'Well, that excludes you then, don't it,' said Mrs O'Gorman.

'Unlike you, I happen to work for my living.'

'Yes, if you can call it that.'

'Keep it up, you mealy-mouthed crab, just you keep it up and – '

'Don't you threaten me.'

'Ladies, please, this is hardly the time and place to – '

'Don't you interfere. This is between me and her.'

Hallam listened, spellbound, until he was distracted by Charisma's dismal voice on the radio. Both the brake release lever and the hand winding wheel were on the missing list. It looked as if vandals had been playing games up there. Hallam swore. There was only one thing for it. Tony Sanderson would have to nip up to the lift motor room in the next block and see if there was a lever and wheel up there that could be used. It was a daunting prospect, right to the top of the next stairway, down again, and right to the top of this one. Tony added his heartfelt curses to the morning's collection.

'And don't you think the council doesn't know about your carryings-on,' came a screech from inside the lift. 'They're on to you all right.'

'*My* carryings-on! I tell you, mister, she's got a sixteen-year-old daughter who's the local bike for every young layabout round here. Had an abortion at fifteen.'

'Why, you . . . you bitch!'

'Her old man's an alky because of the state of her. I mean, you've only got to look at her, she couldn't *pay* a man to sleep with her.'

'Ladies, please . . .' There was a thumping and yelling and the thud of a body against one wall, followed by a more rhythmic pounding on the door. 'For God's sake, help, get me out of here.'

'Don't panic.' Hallam reached up and did his own bit of banging on the door. 'You'll be out soon.'

'That's not panic, it's two birds having a straightener.' Vaseline grinned ruefully. 'I know that sound.'

The struggling and screaming of abuse went on. It was essential to get the occupants out before there was serious bloodshed. Hallam sent Vaseline upstairs to get in to the lift shaft from above and open the door with the mechanism on top of the lift car. The fighting did not slacken even as a gap appeared and the door slid back. Through the opening Hallam had a distorted view of two women in a tangled heap on the floor. Then it was obscured by a man's desperate face thrusting out of the narrow gap. 'Get me out of here – and hurry!'

'Calm down, sir.' Hallam reached up and began to haul the man out on to his left shoulder. There was a moment when he thought the fellow's bottom had stuck, but it came free and he was unceremoniously dumped on to the landing. 'You'll be all right, Mr . . .?'

'Worsley. This is outrageous. I mean, I don't know how I could have been . . . I mean, you don't know . . .'

'Just take a few deep breaths, Mr Worsley, and you'll be fine.'

Worsley obeyed. His first anguished gulps began to take on a normal rhythm. He smiled thankfully. 'I appreciate this. Very much.' He glanced back towards the lift, from which sounds of battle were still being emitted. 'They're totally mad, both of them.' After another minute of measured breathing, he decided to flee the scene and went shakily down the stairs.

Vaseline came back from above as Worsley vanished round the corner of the flight. 'Now there's a man who knows which direction to be moving in.'

They turned their attention to the remaining prisoners. Hallam had to shout at the top of his voice to restore something resembling order. When at last there was silence, apart from some breathing a lot heavier than Worsley's had been, he asked: 'Right, who's first?'

There was no argument. A flushed face with dishevelled hair appeared in the opening. So did a glimpse of a torn blouse and some features which immediately interested Vaseline. Gallantly he stepped forward.

'I think you're going to need a proper fireman's lift, darling.'

The young woman put her tousled head close to his and then wriggled and squeezed herself through the gap. Hallam stepped alongside Vaseline, but Vaseline needed no help. He took the girl's whole weight, appreciating to the full how attractively it was distributed, and gradually lowered her to her feet.

'There are times when I really love this job.'

Hallam said: 'Some small contretemps, was there, madam?'

'What?'

'A misunderstanding of some kind?'

'Oh, no. No misunderstanding. That fat slag attacked me, so I defended myself, right?'

There was a resentful shout from inside. 'Oy, what about me?'

Hallam appraised the situation as Tony Sanderson, by now another heavy breather, panted past him on the way up with a lever and wheel. He was trying to think of something soothing and tactful to say when Vaseline, keeping his arm lightly round the girl on the pretext that she might be feeling dizzy after her ordeal, cried cheerily: 'Afraid you're going to have to hang on for a bit, luv. The gap's not quite, you know . . .'

The girl giggled and said: 'Fat slag.'

Vaseline insisted that while they waited for Tony and the others to free the mechanism way above, he should see her home to her door. They went up two more flights of stairs, Vaseline in the rear so that he could appreciate her calves and the wiggle of her bottom. The experience in the lift did not seem to have done her aplomb a lot of lasting damage. By the time they reached her landing she looked a lot more cheerful, patting her hair into some sort of shape and wiping her smeared lips slowly and caressingly with a tissue.

'Thanks a lot,' she said at her door, but her tone was unhurried and inviting.

'Does your . . . er . . . friend live along this landing as well?'

'If you mean that stinking crab caught down there in the pot yes, more's the pity. There's always one in every block. Crabs with nothing better to do in their miserable lives but spy on people and wallow in gossip.'

'Yeah, these places seem to breed 'em.' said Vaseline, imitating Hallam's manner and tone of voice. 'Anyway, Miss . . . er . . .?'

'Sue.' That was all she was going to give away, for the time being. 'Thanks, anyway.'

'Always ready to help a lady in distress.'

'Ooh, my hero.'

'I'd let you invite me in for a rewarding cup of tea,' said Vaseline, 'but alas, duty calls. Perhaps some other time?'

Her hand on the door, she studied him for a moment. 'Well, I'm sort of married.'

'So am I. Sort of.'

They exchanged lecherous grins of mutual understanding.

It was one of those evenings when, by some unspoken accord, most of Blue Watch drifted off shift and into The Feathers. Vaseline welcomed the opportunity to recount further extravagant versions of his experiences in hospital, followed by a graphic description of the saving of a ravishing beauty from a foul old dragon in a lift. It was a story which would be exaggerated more with each telling.

Josie had left the station ten minutes after the rest of them, taking the opportunity to wash and repair the ravages of the day. Crossing the road, she noticed a woman standing by the bus stop, apparently waiting for the next bus yet gazing fixedly at the fire station – and then at Josie as she approached.

They were only a couple of yards apart when Josie recognized Karen Wilson. Her eyes were oddly glazed, as if she had been swallowing tranquillizers as fast as jelly beans. She tensed as Josie offered an awkward smile and tried to edge past, then threw something at her. Instinctively Josie reached out to catch it and found herself clutching Karen's wedding ring.

Karen had gone quickly away down the street and into the shadows.

Josie stood for a long minute, unsure of whether to brave The Feathers or to go straight home. But if she went home she would be tormented by a snakepit of swirling thoughts. She nerved herself to walk along to the door of the pub and go in.

Tony Sanderson was engaged in a verbal sparring bout with George Green, while Vaseline at the bar expounded upon his prowess with night nurses and as a knight errant. Bayleaf was leaning at the far end, not solitary but well content to keep his distance and listen, disinclined to join in. When he saw Josie he could not repress a warm smile. Then he turned to the barmaid and signalled for a drink, ready and waiting by the time Josie reached him.

Without a word she held out the wedding ring in the palm of her hand. He took it, his contentment fading, and asked a soundless question.

'Outside,' said Josie. 'Not five minutes ago.' As he made a move to leave, she added: 'I think she'll be gone by now.' They drank in silence.

Charisma, trying to make some clumsy sex joke in tune with Vaseline's monologue, realized half-way through that he was making no impact and drifted away with his glass in his hand.

Bayleaf said: 'Look, we've got to . . .' He stopped in mid-sentence and looked past her as the far door from the street swung open, and softly said: 'Oh, shit.'

Josie looked round. She said nothing and did not move, but inside she felt her stomach turning for the second time this evening. Fate was really pushing it a bit hard right now.

Her husband came up to the bar with that insolent, menacing lope which he had always believed made him irresistible and said: 'Sorry to spoil the fun, love, but I'd like to talk to you.'

'Hello, Gerry,' she said warily.

There was a long, uncomfortable pause.

'Well,' said Gerry with a sour glance at Bayleaf, 'can we or can't we?'

Josie looked round at the familiar group. Whatever their faults, whatever the snide remarks, she was one of the team. They were almost too comforting, too predictable, which was more than could ever have been said for Gerry. She was reluctant to leave the warmth of their company. Things outside had been bad enough already. She didn't want to face any further shocks. 'Can't it wait till later?'

The good-natured sparring in the background had begun to die away. Some of the Watch turned to stare, while others made a tactful point of turning away. Either way, it was a blight on the evening.

Gerry waited with that sullen, demanding expression she knew so well. Josie gave up. She pushed her half-empty glass away and turned to follow him out into the street.

7

IN THE light from the pub doorway and windows, Gerry looked unusually smart. This was much the way he had appeared when Josie had first met him: dressed in a casual but well-fitting jacket, a crisp striped shirt with a silk tie, well pressed trousers and suede shoes. And he had recently had his hair styled, making the most of that natural wave which curled down towards his right temple. It was only when they came under the full glare of a street lamp that she could see how his eyes had become puffy and his mouth more bitter and crooked at the corners.

She wondered why he should have come back after all these weeks. It couldn't mean anything good. She wished she could have stayed in The Feathers, but there might have been a scene. Gerry was good at flying off without warning into tempestuous scenes or at the very least of raising his voice into scouring sarcasms. She couldn't have endured that before the rest of the Watch.

'I'll drive us home,' he said, 'and we can talk. Or let's just say' – already there was bitterness close below the surface – 'I'll drive *you* home.'

'I've got the car,' she pointed out.

'Yes. And the flat, and just about everything else.'

Was this what it was all about? Recriminations and backbiting? She had thought there had been enough of that, and it ought to have been all over by now.

He was leading her across the pavement towards a

white Sierra with its panels carrying a gaudy red and blue logo which seemed to have something to do with icicles and camp fires.

'I've got a job,' he went on. 'This is a company car.'

He opened the passenger door for her to get in. She waited until he was settled in the driver's seat before saying, 'Couldn't you have just rung, or called round at the flat, instead of – '

'I did call round. You've changed the locks.'

'Only the Yale. The other one broke.'

'Really?' he said sceptically. 'I can tell you, that nosy old cow upstairs enjoyed every minute of it.'

He started the car and they coasted slowly through the streets she knew off by heart, inside out and every which way. The two of them had driven round them plenty, way back, and shopped along the mall whose lights blazed across the pavement for a moment and then faded away behind them.

Josie said: 'Look, Gerry, what d'you want?'

'I want us to talk.'

'About what?'

'About us. About what's happening.'

'Nothing's happening,' she said bluntly. 'You left, and I'm getting on with my life as best I can.'

His jaw was set and he was staring at the road ahead as if hating every twist and turn, and everyone who crossed it or drove towards him or made him slow down. 'Is that it, then?'

'What d'you expect me to say?'

'You could say, "How's the job, Gerry? Are you happy, Gerry? Have you met someone else, Gerry? Where are you *living*, Gerry?"'

She might have known. The self-pity was nothing new. He had always wanted to be patted on the head for getting a job and bringing in some money, and then to be comforted when he lost a job – which he did with monotonous regularity. Josie had frequently suspected that he lost jobs largely because of his carping self-preoccupation and bouts of sullenness which nobody could overcome; but she had never dared mention it until that final flare-up when they both said just about every lousy thing there was to say. Now that last remark of his showed which way his mind was going this time.

'The flat,' she said dully. 'You want me to sell the flat.'

'You're not listening, Josie.'

'Oh, I'm listening all right.'

'Let me put it another way.' He was not so much pleading as pushing his own irrefutable case and expecting her to give in as a matter of common sense. 'Are *you* happy, Josie? Have *you* met somebody else, Josie? I don't have to ask where you're living, do I, because I *know* where you're living.'

'You've missed one. No "how's the job, Josie?"'

He was silent for a while until he had turned the familiar corner and parked at the kerb outside the familiar front door.

'The job,' he said. Whatever smooth talk he might have planned earlier, he had soon lost his grip on it and was the old Gerry, as familiar as that corner and this front door. 'In the job . . . *on* the job?'

'What is this, Gerry? Do you want to argue, churn out insults, or discuss things? I mean, what the hell are you after?'

He looked at her. She thought he was going to reach out and touch her and prayed he wouldn't. He had stopped staring at the road and now was staring at her and trying to pull himself together. 'I've got work now.'

'Bully for you.'

'Salesman,' he said ingratiatingly. 'Double glazing

company. Don't laugh. I'm getting along all right at it. I've really got the lot of it at my fingertips. And it's work.'

Yes, she had to acknowledge that. It was work. But for how long? In her head she could have done a quick countdown of past pleas and boasts and assurances; but she didn't really need to.

He was impatient for a reply. When none came, he moved on to the next stage of what he had so patently rehearsed. 'I could . . . well, you know, we could . . . you know, try again?'

It was no good looking at him and pretending nothing had ever existed between them. No good despising him; or despising herself for ever having been sweet-talked by such an obvious no-hoper. There had been good times, passionate times, love talk instead of hate talk. He was still handsome, still had that presence, and still had that persuasive voice. Maybe it would persuade lots of people to buy lots of double glazing. Josie was dismally uncertain whether he could actually buy her again – or get her for free.

'I don't know, Gerry.' She slumped down into the car seat. 'I really don't know.'

It was not what he wanted to hear. He had worked out his own lines and could not understand why the responses should not come out, right on cue.

'Too busy screwing firemen, I suppose?'

Josie felt sick inside, but in a way almost relieved. Her judgment had not been wrong. It really would have been stupid to waver and let him get away with it. He didn't want to try anything again, only to scrounge and be admired. And to win every argument. And if things didn't immediately go his way, there was no spitefulness to which he wouldn't stoop.

She opened the car door and began to get out. 'I really don't know,' she said to him. Deep down, actually, she thought that she did know, and had known all along.

She said: 'If you want half the flat, Gerry, get yourself a lawyer.'

He leaned across to pull the door shut, and the venom in his face was what she ought to have expected but which she still, after so many experiences of it, found nauseating.

'Bitch,' he said. 'If that's the way you want it, that's the way it will be.'

She slept badly, telling herself over and over again that she had done her best to keep the marriage together, that it wasn't her fault when things turned sour, and that she was right not to let him coax her into yielding yet again. She had given way before; given him another chance – given both of them another chance – and regretted it. Then regretted the next break-up and fretted and threshed about, tangling with her own conscience. It wasn't her fault, not after so many honest tries. Though it was true, it was not much of a consolation.

And into the middle of her reproaches and worries there swam a picture of Karen Wilson's set, tormented face, and the wedding ring that had lain in Josie's palm.

By the time Blue Watch switched on to the night shift, Vaseline's cheerfulness had partially evaporated. Marion had blithely announced to him that all her dreams were coming true: he was going to be a father.

Vaseline thought of his ex-wives' maintenance money, the bundle he owed the tax man and the cost of electricity and water and everything else in this grasping world. And now there was going to be the additional burden of bringing up a kid, especially if Marion gave up working. Then he thought of the treat he had planned for this first late duty session and brightened up for a while. He was prepared to bet that Sue was not the kind to get pregnant easily.

She was spot on time. After reporting on parade and then disappearing with instructions from Station Officer Tate to check the boxes in the store-room against the latest batch of invoices, he crept cautiously out into the yard and through the doorway into the alley. The battered red Fiat was waiting.

Sue put her head out and let him muss her mouth with a long, suggestive kiss. She looked a lot brighter and readier for action than when he had hauled her out of that lift. He reckoned he could make those legs of hers dance a lot more vigorously than the angry twitch they had given when she was dragged through the opening.

'Right,' she said. 'Where are we going?'

'Not going anywhere.' He opened the back door and jerked his thumb to indicate that she should join him. 'Can't be too far away from the old workplace.'

'You mean . . . here? In my old man's motor?'

'Where else?'

Sue glanced at the fire station. 'What if someone should come out?'

'Well, they won't see us in here if you keep your head down. And everything else.'

Sue hesitated another moment before clambering into the back seat. Vaseline had just settled himself with one arm round her shoulder and was beginning to explore the buttons of her blouse when there was a clangour from the station as the bells went down.

Sue shot upright. 'What's that?'

'Sod it.' Vaseline freed himself and groped for the door handle. 'Don't go away. I'll be back before you know it.'

For once in history he was as good as his word. The shout had taken them only five minutes' drive from the station to find that the call had been a hoax. The buildings supposedly ablaze were in normal condition, and the residents denied all knowledge of any fire alarm.

'Irresponsible bastards,' fumed Hallam on the return journey. Then he clung to the side of the pump cabin as they did a slithering turn round a tight corner. 'Bloody hell, Vaseline. We're coming back off a shout, not going on one.'

'I . . . well, I'm dying to go to the loo, sub.'

The gearbox made a grating, hiccuping sound. The appliance juddered and slowed at the next corner, despite Vaseline's desperation to get back.

Light from the pub on the corner fell on a group half-huddled in the doorway, half-lounging out across the pavement. Four men seemed to be circling two laughing young women, one black and one white. The pale white face turned sharply as the two fire engines came close to the kerb. It was the face of Dorothy Sanderson. Vaseline, grappling with the sticky gear change, found time to wonder if Tony, in the following vehicle, would spot his wife.

Amazing what wives could get up to when their husbands' backs were turned.

Vaseline drove into the station and made an exaggerated show of going to the lavatory. He was out in a few seconds, before anyone else could come in, and sprinted across the yard. The car was still there. So was Sue. She glared at her watch as he arrived.

'About bloody time.'

'False alarm. Would you believe it? Never mind. Make up for lost time.'

Vaseline was not even half-way in through the back door when the bells went down again. It was just too un-bleeding-real.

'Look, don't go away,' he begged. 'Stay there. Got a car radio or anything?'

'Sod this for a lark,' said Sue unromantically.

'Don't start without me. I'll be right back.'

He joined the group in the Appliance room struggling into their gear and waiting for orders. Hallam was dashing towards them with a telex slip, thrusting it at the leading fireman.

Malcolm Cross skimmed the address, then said: 'What's this? Couldn't be. Oh, God, no . . .'

'That sweatshop down the dockside,' snapped Hallam. 'I said from the start we should have rushed that closure order through.'

'Come on.' Malcolm leaped for the pump. 'For God's sake, move it!'

Bayleaf, startled by his intensity, clambered up into the driver's seat, but the pump ladder with Vaseline at the wheel led the way out. The second appliance soon closed the gap. They bellowed their way through the evening streets which were mercifully free of the congestion of daytime traffic. They were approaching the warren of half-derelict streets and shabby warehouses when there was a series of clunks from the engine, and a convulsive juddering shook the whole appliance right through again, only worse than ever this time.

'Come on, Vas,' growled Tate. 'Move it, move it.'

They were slowing to a miserable limp. Vaseline fought to get the appliance in close to the kerb to let Bayleaf and the pump ladder pass. It swung out from behind them, and he caught a glimpse of Malcolm's anguished face, his lips moving as he shouted something; but not a word was audible above the grating of the gearbox.

Tate was banging his fist on the dashboard as if to shove the appliance forward by sheer brute anger. 'Keep it going, you idiot, keep it going.'

'Turn it in, guv,' Vaseline protested. 'Not my fault, is it?'

Tate reached for the radio phone and began summoning urgent back-up. Vaseline urged the crippled vehicle on, cursing and at the same time praying. Neither the curses nor the prayers seemed to be doing any good.

Flames and smoke were pouring from the first-floor windows. The rickety main staircase was already ablaze and the fire exit was locked, in spite of what Malik had been told. Nobody was fighting a way out from that end.

Malcolm looked desperately back along the street. What the hell was the matter with them? Where the hell was that pump?

There was a wave of wild screaming from above. A girl with a sari alight, engulfing her in a shroud of flame, came tumbling down the stairs and rolled into the street. Josie Ingham threw herself forward and began to hose the girl down. Malcolm tried to heave a hose towards the stairs, just as they collapsed in great gouts of fire and sparks. Desperately he waved to Tony Sanderson to follow him as he ran down the alley beside the building. They went up the shaky, rusty fire escape to the still-locked fire exit. The screams inside were becoming unbearable. The nearest window suddenly cracked with the heat, and a howling human torch tried to climb out, then seemed hideously to be sucked back in again.

Tony began axing his way through the fire exit. At last it gave way and he pulled the flaps open. Malik was the first out, whimpering, pushed towards the steps by a rush of choking, scorched and smoke-blinded girls. Malcolm tried to steady them, directing them down one by one, staring into every face as it passed him. No Samina. Not yet. But there had to be. She had to fight her way out any moment now.

Below him at last the pump lurched into position at

the end of the alley. There was the distant wail of an ambulance, and an auxiliary fire engine called in by Tate was manoeuvring towards the main door.

A ladder swung up beside Malcolm on the fire escape. A hose swung at an angle and began cutting a swathe through the roaring inferno within. He took three steps into the room, feeling the floor starting to crumble beneath his feet. He shouted insanely. 'Samina . . . Samina . . .?' The roar of the flames mockingly drowned out his voice and the screams of what lay beyond. He stumbled against something. It was a charred, still-smouldering body, unrecognizable. And the dark, crumpled lumps beyond the next line of flames would all be unrecognizable before this was finished. It was too late for any of them to fight or claw their way out.

When the hellish sounds of blazing destruction had been fought down and subdued to an evil, intermittent crackling, there were no sounds of human voices left. No words from Samina; only echoes in Malcolm Cross's mind.

He slumped on the pump fender, refusing to believe it. When Josie came to stand beside him, her hand very lightly on his shoulder, he was hardly aware of her. Or of Tate, coming anxiously towards him and then catching Josie's eye and turning away.

Tony Sanderson made his way home wearily through the grey, overcast morning. He thought he was hardened to the worst that could happen at the scene of a fire, but tonight's work had been worse than most he could remember. He was drained. Any other time he would have been glad to get home, put his arms round Dorothy, and collapse into a few hours of forgetful sleep. That was the only way to cope with the sort of things they saw and had to do in this job. But tonight it couldn't be like that; not after what he had seen outside the pub. The miseries of it were not yet over.

He dragged himself up the stairs to the landing and paused for a long moment outside his own front door. Then he forced himself to go in.

Normally Dorothy would have been in bed. Any fireman's wife who sat up anxiously waiting for his homecoming would soon die of exhaustion. But this morning she was awake and dressed and obviously had not been to bed yet.

'Tone.' She tried to put her arms round him, but he wasn't having any of that.

'Enjoy yourself last evening?'

'Tone, it was only me and Jenny going out for a couple of hours, like we used to.'

'When you were out looking for a feller?'

'We never went out looking for fellers.'

'You sure found some last night.'

'I know what you must've been thinking, Tony, but it was all completely innocent, honest. We just had these drinks, and a few blokes tried to chat us up. We just thought it was funny.'

'Funny?'

Dorothy made another move towards him. 'Honest, we just walked off and made an early night of it.'

He went towards the bedroom door. He was so tired that her face was no more than a blur.

'I gotta get some sleep.' He went into the bedroom and closed the door.

8

SHE CAME into the bar with the tinkle of a charm
bracelet and dangling earrings, and a sharp tap
of high heels on the floor. There was a bird picked
out in blue and silver sequins on her left breast, and
a buckle bright with fake diamonds at the top of her
short black skirt. Charisma, brooding over his drink,
looked at her as she walked in, then looked again,
and then looked away. He had still not recovered from
that Lonely Hearts encounter which had turned out so
creepy. Uneasily he knew that there must be a picture of
himself in his fireman's uniform on that weird woman's
wall. His only consolation was that there was probably
one of George Green in a chauffeur's cap and tightly
buttoned jacket. On the whole, he was not in the mood
to chat up any other woman. This pub was his local
and he wanted to keep it the way it was, separate
from anything else in his life. A quiet pint, and then
home. That was the pattern, and it was going to stay
that way.

There was the scrape of a stool as she edged along the
bar closer to him.

'Hang about.' She clicked her fingers. 'I know you.
Fireman . . . er . . .'

'Appleby.'

'I'm Donna.' When he looked blank she trilled an
arch little twitter. 'Remember Liver Salts – was made
up and went to Kilburn?'

He had to look full at her now. She had very wide,

innocent eyes and a pert little mouth. She could be anything up to thirty, but the skin at her throat was young and smooth. When she leaned forward slightly, as if hanging on whatever he would say next, he could see that it went on being smooth quite a way down.

'You're not Mrs Liver Salts?' he ventured.

'No, it wasn't quite like that.' She looked down coyly and stroked her right knee. Charisma watched the gliding, rhythmic movement; hypnotized. 'I was his Common Law. We was shacked up together for five years. We was going to tie the knot, but we never.' Donna raised her eyes again, and her sharp little East End voice softened into a respectful coo. 'We was never introduced, you and me, but I remember seeing you a lot in The Feathers.'

'Me and the lads get in there quite frequent,' Charisma nodded.

'Yeah.' The voice was sharp again. 'Liver Salts spent his life there when he wasn't at the station. Five years I played bleeding second fiddle to Blue Watch, a couple of fire engines and a pub.' She glanced at the clock behind the bar. 'You're not on your way in, are you?'

'No, I'm at the end of my four days off. On again tomorrow.' Although she had not made any further move, he felt that somehow they were drawing closer together. 'Can I get you a drink?'

'I'll have a double gin and lime,' said Donna promptly.

Conrad, the barman, had been watching the two of them with some interest. As he poured the drink he said: 'How'd the karate thingee go?'

'Sorry?' For a moment Charisma was baffled.

'The karate thingee the other night. You said you was going in for some competition.'

Now Charisma remembered. He must have had a skinful, sounding off like that last Thursday. 'Right.'

He had no choice but to go on with it now. 'Terrific, yeah. I got me black belt.'

'Congratulations.' Conrad was genuinely impressed. He pushed the gin and lime towards Donna and poured Charisma another pint. 'Have these on me.'

Charisma looked guiltily into his beer, not sure what it was safe to talk about next. As Conrad moved away to serve another customer, Donna said quietly:

'I was looking for accommodation.' When she was sure she had got his attention, she went on: 'A bedsit, anything. See, when me and Liver Salts split, I moved in with me sister. But her old man's after me. You know, give him half a chance and he'd be in there like a ferret.'

Charisma felt himself blushing and buried his nose in his glass.

'And our Shirl thinks it's me what's leading him on,' said Donna tragically. 'I says, leave it out, I says. I'd rather be embraced by a sodding boa-constrictor.'

'Shirl?'

'Me sister.'

Her perfume, a sort of rich orange and honeysuckle scent, was beginning to envelop Charisma. He looked down at her knee, so close to his hand; and the gentle bulges beneath the silver bird and the sequins. Hoarsely he said: 'It's not your fault you're attractive. But I mean . . . your sister's husband . . .'

She put a hand on his arm and looked up into his eyes with a hopeful smile. 'Maybe you should teach me karate?'

She had emptied her glass pretty quickly. He bought her another drink. She sighed and looked at her watch; and after another long sigh she said: 'I suppose I'll have to go back and face it. Until I can find some little place on my own.'

He heard himself saying: 'Care for a cup of coffee

before you call it a day?' Five minutes later he found himself walking back with her to the terrace in the little backstreet that had been home for as long as he could remember.

While he tipped instant coffee grains into two mugs, he heard her moving about the living-room. It was odd: she wasn't just idly inspecting things, but somehow sounded steady and purposeful. But her smile when he came in with the coffee mugs was still shy and deferential. She pointed to the cups and medallions on the sideboard.

'What's that, at the end?'

'Snooker trophy.'

'And the others?'

'Oh, darts, and golf – and that one's for squash.'

He had bought them in a run-down sports shop down the Old Kent Road and polished them so that they made a super display, with a strip light above them. His mother had laughed when he had brought them home, but never actually criticized him.

'You're quite a sportsman,' said Donna.

It was nice to be looked up to by a bird who looked like this. He couldn't believe the evening was really going to go on the way he would like it to. He had long ago forgotten the kinky Nicola. Here was the real thing.

'Where's your black belt?' she asked.

'Aw . . . er . . . no, I haven't got that yet. See, they have to measure you for it and send off for it, in case it might not fit.'

She sat down in his usual armchair and crossed her legs, tugging her skirt a fraction higher. 'So you're more or less on your lonesome, then, just like me.'

'Well, yeah. Loads of mates, like.' Charisma perched on the edge of the couch. 'It's rare I'm in.'

'But you live alone?'

'Since Mum went, yeah.'

'Oh, I'm sorry.'

'It was a blessed release, really. She'd had bad legs and a gall bladder for years.'

Donna got up and began strolling round the little room again, sizing it up. He was glad he had tidied up before going out. He liked to keep the place looking its best, even when there was nobody but himself to see it. That was how he had been brought up. He was proud of what Donna must be seeing: a nice cosy little place, worth quite a bit now that the area had come up – becoming gentrified, as some of the older neighbours said.

Donna stood above him. 'I can't keep calling you Fireman Appleby.'

'Leslie.'

'Leslie. That's nice.' She lowered herself to the couch beside him and put her head on his shoulder. Her hand began to move across his lap. 'You're very shy, aren't you, Leslie?'

Josie had taken the third wrong turning of the evening to find herself in the middle of a pottery class. Even the teacher did not seem to know where in the building the other adult education classes took place. She backed out and prepared to start again.

'Excuse me.' Someone spoke behind her. 'I'm looking for the Spanish for Beginners.'

He was a man of middle height and, she estimated, early middle age, wearing a pin-striped dark blue suit and a very clean shirt. There was a puckish sort of grin in his eyes, as if he was always expecting strange mishaps to occur.

'So am I,' she said. 'But I've no idea where it is, either.'

They laughed. His eyes darted this way and then that,

and he spread his hands apologetically. 'Since it seems as though we're going to be classmates, shall we look for it together?'

They reached a T-junction of corridors. Josie had already tried the long corridor to the left, so suggested the one to the right this time. It proved right in both senses of the word. They arrived at the door of the Spanish class just as everyone else had settled behind the chipped, inkstained desks.

From time to time during that first session she caught the man's curious gaze on her. It was not difficult to ignore him. She had lots of things on her mind, and getting involved with another man was not one of them. Divorce proceedings against Gerry were going to be very messy, there was no doubt about that. And when it was all over, she fancied a holiday on the Costa del Sol; which was why she was here. Silly, really. She would never learn Spanish seriously or study it in depth; but at least she wanted to acquire a smattering so that she could detach herself for a short time from London and Gerry and Blackwall Fire Station and every other drab, dispiriting thing in her life.

It would be nice if Bayleaf could come with her. It was a wayward, wanton thought she dismissed fiercely from her mind. The vision of that wedding ring and Karen's obsessed face still scorched her memory. No more men for Josie Ingham for a long, long time yet.

At the end of the session she found a canteen in the building which was only marginally more stimulating than the fire station mess. As she sipped her coffee she was aware of someone drifting across the room, and knew resignedly who it had to be.

He sat down and said: 'Just for the record, my name's David.'

'Josephine. Josie to my friends.'

'Maybe I could be included in those?'

112

She was sorry now that she had put it that way. But he looked a civilized type, a trifle sheepish and in any case harmless. Conversation over teacups committed you to nothing.

'Not a very sociable group, our Spanish class,' he said. 'Nobody else staying on for the tea and the mutual sympathy.'

'Perhaps everyone will get more sociable when we all know one another better. After all,' she said pointedly, 'I suppose a lot of the women have baby-sitters and most of the men have wives to go home to.'

'I haven't.'

Some instinct had already told her that. It was strange. He was quite good-looking, well-dressed, and had a suave, easygoing manner. Yet his eyes had that strange evasiveness. And what was someone with so much apparently going for him doing at elementary Spanish classes in bleak school buildings on the fringes of the East End?

He was studying her with his head on one side, not unlike a well-groomed parrot, wanting a personal disclosure to match his own.

'No,' she informed him crisply, 'I don't have a wife to go home to, either.'

He smiled that lopsided smile of his. It could be disturbing; or attractive. It was getting too late in the evening for her to decide on that. With difficulty she suppressed a yawn.

'I'm an accountant,' he said. 'How about you?'

'Firefighter. London Fire Brigade.'

As he was registering surprise and obviously seeking for an appropriate response, she looked at her watch and grabbed up her handbag.

'So you're what's known as an emancipated woman.'

'Yes, I suppose I am.'

'So there's no point in my offering you a lift home?'

'Definitely not. See you next week.'

'*Buenos noches*,' he said.

His accent sounded authentic enough after a first lesson. She did not feel confident enough to try and match him with a fluent reply.

'Goodnight.'

The demolition job had been raising dust and protests for more than three weeks now. Vaseline had come close to it only in the past week, but was already suffering from a sore throat and aching eyes. He would rather not have spent his days off in the same smothering atmosphere he knew only too well from brigade duties, only without breathing apparatus. But the news that he was to be a father and that Marion would eventually have to stop working in the supermarket, on top of the arrears he owed his earlier wives, had made it all too plain that he needed a moonlighting career alongside the miserable one hundred-and-fifty poxy quid he took home from his fire service each week.

He was not too keen on the way Big Eddie talked to him, or the way Big Eddie bossed him around and snarled at him. But Eddie's roofing jobs paid well, and in between-whiles he could fit in some quick private jobs to raise a few more quid here, a backhander there. The grit from the warehouses as they came down bit by bit blew across the rooftops; but it was a lot less suffocating than some of the things he inhaled when hacking his way into similar warehouses in the process of burning down or falling down around his earholes.

Taking a surreptitious break round the corner from Eddie's latest job, he watched three or four winos tottering out of a warehouse scheduled for swift demolition. A couple of good-tempered policemen shepherded them away from the site, watching like well-trained dogs to make sure they did not weave round and return. One winked matily at Vaseline, obviously remembering his face but not able to place him.

A young workman leaning on a road drill watched the winos totter away in search of a handout to buy refreshment. 'I get nightmares that I've buried those buggers alive.'

The nearest police constable grinned. 'You'd have performed a public service, squire.'

Vaseline wiped his eyes. They were smarting more than usual. There was something more than dust in the air, but he couldn't place it. Around this shambles, it could be anything: decaying winos, or something nasty uncovered as walls came down and basements were dug out.

'Hoi!' It was Eddie's irate summons. He was a big man and he had a big bellow. He paid out happily enough when work had been done the way he wanted it, but he could be a savage taskmaster if things were not going exactly the way he wanted them. He always wore a blue knitted cap which could have made him look silly. But nothing and nobody would ever dare to make Big Eddie look silly. He had a way of turning the tables and making his opponent look very foolish indeed, if not downright pulverized. 'You doing this job, or not?'

'I'll just nip down to the post office and pay my money in,' said Vaseline ingratiatingly. 'Thanks a lot, Eddie. Won't be more than a few minutes.'

'Don't you stitch me up.'

'No, Foxtrot Oscar,' Vaseline mumbled under his breath.

He wondered just how he could fit in that window repair job for the Italian eaterie down the road with completing Eddie's roofing job on schedule. The young wife of the bloke running the café was dark and delicious, a real stunner. But Eddie could do a bit of stunning on his own. It was a rough old life, with precious few perks, and every one of those hedged round with prickles.

Vaseline sniffed at that seeping, intrusive smell. The sooner he was finished in this atmosphere, the better.

The teleprinter slip announced a suspicious outbreak of smoke from the crossroads in the middle of the Wharf Flats conversion area. The gas board had been notified, but said there were no gas mains in the neighbourhood. By the time Station Officer Tate and the pump had racketed their way down the wharf road with their two tones blaring, a ragged hole in the road had been cordoned off by the police. At the junction with the main road they were busy setting up diversion signs for traffic.

'Okay, get back.' George Green shouldered his way through the usual crowd of rubberneckers. Even if they had been told the world was about to go up in smoke and they would lose at least their hair and eyebrows, and maybe a lot more, there would always be a crowd just like this. 'Get back. Let's get some light on this.'

Wisps of smoke were curling up from the hole. It looked far from threatening, but there was no telling.

'Lot worse ten minutes ago,' a voice from the edge of the throng volunteered.

Tate and Green advanced cautiously. The conflagration, such as it was, seemed to have been caused by a lighted match dropped on to a heap of rubbish. The rubbish itself must have been tossed in by someone on the way back from a takeway: not so much a storm in a teacup as a threatened blaze in a Kentucky Fried Chicken box.

'That hole's been there for ages,' said a woman on

the edge of the pavement. 'My old man had a skinful the other night, fell in and lost a tooth.'

'Stand back then, love,' said George morosely, 'and when we've finished we'll have a look for it.'

The two of them had just stood back from the hole when something hard hit Tate on the back of his helmet. As he ducked instinctively, there was another clang against its rim. Two soup cans rolled across the road in front of him.

He looked up irately, and narrowly missed getting a third can in his face. The fusillade increased, with full and empty cans showering around them or missing and bouncing along the pavement.

'You bastards!' The yell came from a third floor window. 'I didn't get to bed till nine o'clock, you noisy swine.'

Tate dodged another can and yelled back: 'You cut that out, laddie, or I'll break your flaming neck!'

The only answer was a handful of eggs breaking and splashing at his feet. The rubberneckers who had been clustered near the hole in the road turned their attention to this fresh bit of entertainment and set about throwing some of the cans back. From this angle they were more likely to break somebody else's windows than hit the attacker.

'Yell for the Bill, guv,' George Green advised, ducking as a can ricocheted from a windowsill.

Tate jerked a thumb for Malcolm Cross to follow him. Automatically Malcolm lifted a fire extinguisher from the appliance, and the two of them marched into the building and up the stairs. An elderly woman on the third landing put her head nervously out and nodded at the neighbouring door, then darted back inside. They heard the key turn in the lock. Tate began to pound on the door she had indicated.

It was flung back. A youngish-middle-aged ragged

man in a sweat-stained T-shirt stood in the doorway. He had not shaved for a couple of days, and his hair was as wild as his eyes. 'You want some more?' he raged, thrusting his head forward. 'Come and get it, if you want it.'

'Now you and me are going inside' – Tate and Malcolm Cross took the man's arms and steered him back into the room – 'and we're going to have a nice sit-down and a chat, laddie.'

In the main room of the flat they stopped, taken aback. The whole place was piled high with boxes from floor to ceilings. There were crates of tinned food, some labelled as dried milk, and trays of eggs. In the corner was an Elsan toilet. Worst of all, on the restricted space left on a table lay two shotguns.

Tate squeezed past a teetering mound of boxes and slammed the window shut.

'Now, just what is this caper? You expecting a siege, or what?'

'It's for after the holocaust.' The man seemed surprised that any explanation was necessary. 'The nuclear holocaust. A group of us have pooled our resources and are building a bunker in Staines. It's been my turn to work on it at nights.' His voice rose to the volume they had heard from the window. 'But it's been impossible to get any sleep round here. It's been the Council with pneumatic drills for weeks, and now you lot and your bloody sirens.'

'Now look, mate . . .'

The anger faded as quickly as it had blown up. 'We're just a group of like-minded people, hell-bent on survival – on the survival of the human race. All of us males have frozen our sperm.'

Footsteps clumped along the landing. Malcolm stood back to let a police constable into the room.

The man backed away as far as he could go, which

was not far. He flattened himself against one of his barricades of boxes. 'It's in the fridge,' he said plaintively. 'There's no law against it, is there?'

The policeman was eyeing the guns. 'No law against what?'

Vaseline quit the Italian eaterie with regret. He had managed to slip in that job at double speed, allowing a few minutes to have a cup of coffee and chat up the girl to some effect. There wasn't much left to do on the window frames, but he promised he would be back, and he would allow more time for discussion next time. It was only after he had torn himself away from the spell of those dark eyes and was cycling back to the roofing job that he began to think again about Big Eddie, who was more into the world of black eyes and colourful bruises.

The job had not made much progress in his absence. Nor had Eddie's temper improved. The roof was almost stripped of slates, but Mrs Baldock, the owner of the house, did not seem much impressed by progress so far.

'How much longer are you going to be?'

'Look, I can't get on.' You could hear Eddie's bellow from the far end of the street. 'Ain't got no Oppo, have I?'

Vaseline pedalled more swiftly, and propped his bike against the wall.

'Everything okay?'

'No, everything is not okay,' seethed Eddie. 'Where the hell have you been?'

'I told you. The post office. Only there was a queue.'

'All morning?'

'It was a long queue.' Vaseline tried to look alert and ready for hard work. 'Where's the scaffolding?' He looked up at the front of the building and realized Eddie had never had any intention of squandering money on scaffolding. One ladder, and that was it. It wasn't even a good ladder. One side was shorter than the other, so its foot was propped up by a block of wood. 'No,' said Vaseline. 'I'm not going up no manquee ladder.'

Eddie grabbed him by the collar. 'You are supposed to be a wanking fireman.'

'I'm off duty, mate.'

'Now listen.' This close, Eddie's breath was pretty ferocious. It wouldn't have taken much to set it alight. 'You've had your sub. Now sodding well get up there.'

Vaseline got up there.

He was given no chance of slipping away for the rest of the day. By the time he lowered himself cautiously down the ladder for the last time, his knees were aching from kneeling on that roof and his hands were raw. Eddie was still glowering and still suspicious.

'If you don't show up on time tomorrow – '

'Up with the lark,' said Vaseline chirpily.

He was in no mood for larks of any kind, really. By the time he had cycled home his knees and calf muscles were worse and he was only just capable of tottering into the living-room and switching on the television. He groped for half a cigarette from behind his ear as Marion came in with a pile of dirty washing in her arms.

'Oh, you do come home.'

'No, I'm on a frigging world cruise, ain't I?' he muttered under his breath.

But she had heard him. Tears came to her eyes. They seemed to come very readily nowadays. 'Yes, it would have been nice.'

'What would?'

'A honeymoon,' she wailed.

Vaseline sank back and watched the meaningless flickers on the screen. She would have to start the moment he got in, wouldn't she? And there was no telling when she would stop. He didn't even have the energy to stop her the way he had managed to up till now.

Charisma almost regretted not having been out on that particular shout. Malcolm's graphic account of the prophet of disaster made it sound a whole lot different from most of their routine operations.

'Of course,' Charisma said knowledgeably, 'sperm banks are big business in the States, you know. You can make a bomb.'

George looked up from his plate of spaghetti. 'Who can?'

'Well, men can.' Charisma fidgeted. He didn't like the way they were all smirking at him. 'Well, geniuses can.'

'No danger of any sperm being sold from around this table, then,' said Josie dryly.

Malcolm, who had livened up during the telling of the incident, was sinking back into the gloom that had possessed him ever since the sweatshop fire. He looked at Josie almost as if he hated her; or maybe hated to look at or listen to any woman. 'Some of us,' he growled, 'don't have any to sell.'

It was high time to drift away from the table. Charisma, still in a mood to talk and anxious to confide in someone or at any rate to start a long process of hinting, followed Mike Wilson into the kitchen.

'Bayleaf, could I have a word with you when you've got a minute?'

'About what?'

'Well, let's just say a personal matter.' He tried a sly wink, but it did not get across.

'About your B.O., is it?' Bayleaf said.

Maggie squirted washing-up liquid into the sink. This

121

really wasn't a good time or place to discuss intimate matters.

He waited until they were in the Appliance room washing down the pump, and tried again.

'Bayleaf, you're a man.'

'Last time I looked, yeah.'

'Ever felt it was love at first sight?'

It was difficult to explain. The suddenness of it, the wonder of it. He remembered Donna's little round face and the eagerness with which she had wrapped those smooth legs round him, and the things she had lovingly whispered. But how could you put this across and share the happiness with anyone else? Of course, he had shared plenty with the lads. Good times and rough times. And a pretty hectic sporting and social life . . .

No. It was one thing trying to put that across to keep folk thinking he was quite a character – folk like the barman in his local. But in fact he had always been a bit of a loner. And since Mum had dropped off the twig he hadn't confided much in anybody; not much that was true, anyway. Now the urge to communicate, and hear Bayleaf's approval, was overpowering. 'Looking into someone's eyes one night,' he sighed, 'and thinking yes, this is what it's all about. Ever since me Mum died – '

Bayleaf began to register. 'Hang about.' He turned off the hose and looked quizzically at Charisma. 'When did all this happen?'

'Last night. That's what I wanted to talk to you about.'

'Your Mum died last night?'

'No,' said Charisma hurriedly. 'That's not what I meant. I mean, *that* was last winter.'

'You never said.'

In fact, Charisma remembered dismally, he had told them about it but it hadn't registered. Station Officer

Tate had given him compassionate leave; and the S.O. and Mrs Tate had been the only ones at the funeral. It was on the same day as the Brigade cup final with British Rail. He had bravely said to the undertaker that normally it would have taken an earthquake to keep the lads away.

'She wasn't actually me Mum,' he confessed. 'She was me Nan.' Answering Bayleaf's puzzled frown, he went on: 'I called her Mum because she brung me up. But me Mum I called me sister, kinda thing. She got spliced when I was thirteen and emigrated.' He paused, conscious of having revealed things he had never meant to come out with. 'Don't tell the lads.'

'You got any idea who your old man was?' asked Bayleaf sympathetically.

'No, but I've been thinking of making enquiries.' Charisma could not resist it. 'I seem to remember her saying something about someone with a title.'

Bayleaf's sympathy gave way to scepticism. And still Charisma had not told him what he had started out to say.

Never mind. They would all know soon enough. He could spring it on the lot of them one day when the atmosphere was right. There'd be some good-humoured joshing, but when they saw Donna there'd be a lot of envy. He could just imagine their faces.

He was eager for the Watch to end: eager to get home, get ready, and take up where they had left off in the early hours of this morning. He wanted to be sure it was real. He still found it hard to believe that it had happened so suddenly, out of the blue, and so perfectly.

The sound of the cab arriving brought him to the front door, opening it, ready to throw his arms round Donna.

She teetered up the short path, a black plastic mac loosely arranged over her shoulders, struggling with an

123

armful of supermarket bags and a transparent dress bag.

'I ain't got enough for the cab, Leslie.'

He forked out a tenner, and gave her a hand with her belongings. Bags, suitcases, two gaudy lamps, some pink cushions and a pink hair-dryer went in through that front door, which had never seen things quite like this. Donna arrayed a whole family of soft toys, from a tiny koala bear to a huge Snoopy, in the living-room, and found a vase for a sheaf of plastic flowers.

'Stick the kettle on for us, Leslie, while I nip upstairs.'

He heard her thumping about above, and was a bit uneasy about the direction of that noise. As the kettle began to sing, he went up to the landing and through the open door at the top. Donna was spreading an imitation leopard-skin bed cover over the duvet and two frilled pillows.

Charisma gulped. 'This is Mum's room.'

'It's the only double bed in the house.'

'But she died in it.'

Donna let herself sprawl back on the cover, opening her arms and rustling her stockinged knees together. 'Leslie,' she said softly, 'life must go on.'

9

THE YOUNG workman who had been agitated about the demolition of the old warehouse site was a whole lot more agitated now. When the pump arrived and Hallam got down beside the policeman who had phoned in with the emergency call, there was only an impressive heap of rubble, like something out of a film about the Blitz. The final stages of demolition had required no manpower: the whole building had decided to dissolve of its own accord.

A bedraggled woman who could have been any age between thirty and sixty made a wavering circuit of the ruins. Every time she came near anyone else they stepped back. She gave off a reek that itself would have rotted the foundations of a tower block, thought Hallam; a decrepit, foul female equivalent of his stinking father-in-law.

He forced himself to ask the routine questions crisply and formally.

The workman, shifting nervously from one foot to the other, said: 'I did warn one of your lot. And that old bag over there' – he nodded at the wandering woman wino – 'she reckons some of her mates is under there. She slept in there with 'em last night.'

The woman realized they were talking about her and shuffled ingratiatingly closer. 'I only went out this morning to buy some new tights. When I come back it wasn't there no more. And the rest of 'em, I reckon there's the lot of 'em under that. And all my gear. All my gear's in there. Who do I sue?'

Hallam briefly inspected her lumpy legs. Whatever she had bought this morning, it seemed unlikely that it had been a new pair of tights.

'You sure about this, are you, madam?' And to the workman he said: 'How many do you reckon there could be under there?'

The young man shrugged nervously. There was no way he wanted to commit himself.

'Whereabouts do you reckon they are?' When there was still no answer, Hallam stared despondently across the expanse of rubble and girders. Out of the corner of his eye he was aware of the woman wiping her lips as if to make another attempt to bend his ear. With nothing and nobody else to pick on, he abruptly exploded: 'Sicknote, get that woman out of here.'

Josie and Malcolm exchanged glances. That father-in-law problem was making the sub more and more tetchy.

Hallam had finished his assessment. They were going to need a lot of help to dig through this mess: not their own pump ladder, since a ladder was the last thing you needed to claw down through the debris, but a Forward Control vehicle and some experts with a heat-seeking camera. The messages went out; and by the time the rescue team had assembled it had also acquired a police car and a police dog van.

There was little chance, thought Hallam glumly, of anyone surviving beneath the crushing weight and jagged edges of that warehouse. But he watched as the dogs prowled over the rubble and the camera began probing, willing them to smell or distinguish a sign of life. There had to be a voice somewhere, a movement, *something*.

An assistant district officer reached the corner of the

site in a red Maestro and began hauling his fire gear out of the boot. After only the briefest consultation with Hallam he took charge and began barking orders. The fire crews set about carefully moving bricks and girders with their bare hands.

Another car disgorged a newspaper reporter and a cameraman. They waited with ghoulish greed for something to appear – preferably something nasty.

'Sir!'

Everyone tensed and there was silence. Bricks stayed in the men's hands. A man with a shovel leaned on it as if waiting to dig an instant grave.

'Found something?' whispered the A.D.O.

'Thought we heard a tapping noise down there.'

They listened. It lasted forever, the silence and the waiting. But the silence was not going to be broken. There was no further sound, if there had ever been one. Men resumed work, picking and sifting and crawling across the ragged battlefield. Twenty minutes of painstaking, backbreaking work went on; thirty minutes; forty minutes. And no sound or suspicion of life from beneath.

At Hallam's elbow a blurred voice said: 'You couldn't spare us a couple of quid, could yer, guv?'

He waved his hand dismissively without looking round, but the young workman who had raised the alarm made a wild hop across the rubble and slithered to a halt. 'Where did you spring from?'

The tattered wino gave him a sly leer. 'County Sligo.'

All at once there was a whole troop of them, lurching across the site from the street. Two of the men were clutching bottles of what looked like meths, while two of the women clung to each other and managed to stay roughly upright as they made for the centre of the scene.

The A.D.O. glared at Hallam, who hardly dared return his gaze.

Josie and Malcolm began to chuckle. It was the first time Malcolm had looked capable of amusement since that awful night of Malik's inferno. It was silly laughter – the laughter of strain suddenly released, the knowledge that nobody was hurt and the whole thing had been a non-starter.

'All right, all right.' A policeman was herding people back across the roadway. 'There's nothing to see.'

'I take it,' said the A.D.O. bleakly, 'that that unsavoury little lot is the persons who are supposed to be buried alive?'

Hallam was going red and threatening to turn purple. 'Must be, sir.'

'Turned into something of a fiasco, hasn't it?'

'Sir.'

'Put a stop to it. And fast.'

Wretchedly Hallam turned towards his team. Before he could speak, their own pump ladder came rolling up on the outskirts of the watchers. Tate dismounted and consulted the A.D.O. Then, his face set, he came walking towards the sub.

The other members of the Watch seemed to melt away, finding urgent tasks to do.

Tate planted himself in front of Hallam, hands on his hips. 'You're real station officer material, you are, John. Only six E.T.'s in the entire area covered by the London Brigade. That's six hundred and twenty square miles and over seven and a half million people, and you call out the whole cavalry on the say-so of some woman who's probably got so much meths in her blood stream that if you struck a match by her she'd go up in a sheet of blue flame.'

For Tate it was such an uncharacteristically ranting outburst that Hallam was speechless. Before he could even sort out a possible answer, his S.O. grated: 'Well, what are you waiting for – the Queen's Award for Cock-ups?'

Glumly they drove back to Blackwall. No feeling of accomplishment, of a job well done. Not this time.

One thing that was carefully concealed from either Tate or Hallam before they got back was the presence in the TV room of a young woman. Or, as Maggie acidly referred to her, a tart. She had airily asked for Fireman Appleby, and when told that he was out on a shout had said it was all right, she knew her way around the station and she'd wait for him. Maggie had not liked the attitude – mental or physical. But at least she had spared Charisma the wrath of the S.O. and his sub, which today of all days was just as well. She had shunted Charisma quickly down the corridor and he had blanched at the sight of Donna on these hallowed premises, although he let her glue her lips to his.

'Angel,' he said fondly, 'you're not supposed to come into a fire station without proper authority.'

'But you didn't leave me any money this morning, Leslie. I can't do no shopping or nothing.'

Charisma caught a glimpse of George Green's incredulous face at the window in the door of the TV room. Then it was gone. He would have to do some explaining later, and he was quite looking forward to it.

He fumbled in his pocket and handed over a couple of crumpled tenners.

'I'll have something special waiting for you tonight,' said Donna huskily. 'You'll be straight back, won't you? I don't want no more of that hanging around in pubs. Not no more.'

Of course he would hurry back. There was a lot to hurry back for now. No longer an empty house and the need to get his own grub. No more hanging about in

pubs. Only he did intend to have just half an hour in
The Feathers. After George had blabbed what he had
seen, they would simply have to be told the truth.

There was a less than romantic moment when Sub
Officer Hallam, in a foul temper, passed Charisma on
the stairs and sniffed. 'What've you got on?'

'After shave,' said Charisma proudly.

'Since early this morning?'

'It's good stuff. My bird gave it to me.'

Hallam paused to look at his hair. 'Toyed with your
barnet and all, did she?'

Coming up behind him, an equally livid Station
Officer Tate roared: 'You look a right bender. Get
something done about that. This is a working fire
station, not the Royal bleeding Ballet.'

The spell of unpleasantness was a bit hurtful, but had
not lasted long enough to disturb the groundswell of
Charisma's euphoria. He preened himself and prepared
for a half-hour of stunning revelations.

The revelations stunned Bayleaf even before Charisma
arrived in the pub. He had just settled at a table with
Josie, tactfully allowing Tony Sanderson to sit between
them, when George Green arrived with a pint tankard
and slammed it down on their table.

'You heard about Charisma's tart?'

'A sort of vague suggestion,' said Bayleaf, remembering Charisma's confused meanderings.

'You *seen* her?'

'Not yet.'

'Oh, but you have. Way back. Would you believe –
Donna?'

'Thought you said she was a tart, not a kebab.'

'Donna,' said George fiercely. 'Liver Salts's old Common Law.'

This time Bayleaf felt the message go icily home. He

130

spluttered on a mouthful of bitter and put his glass down. Malcolm, coming to join them, stood frozen for a moment. There was quite a chill factor in the bar.

Before they could say any more, Charisma came in, trying to look urbane but dying for someone to make some kind of remark. He bought only half a pint of lager. Obviously he had no intention of staying for long. Or maybe he was frightened to risk staying.

Bayleaf looked at that complacent expression and felt even worse about the whole set-up. 'In a bit of a hurry tonight?'

'Yeah, as it happens.' Charisma stood close to the table, sipping rather than drinking his lager. 'Birds,' he said dreamily. 'They can't half get to you in the nicest possible way.'

'Taking her out on the town, are we?'

'Well, actually, she's knocking us up a paella tonight.'

George made no attempt to conceal his horror. 'She's not moved into your gaff, has she?'

'Well, we both thought that was the adult thing to do, under the circumstances, 'cos it's been getting a bit . . . well, you know . . .' He waved his glass airily but perilously.

'Fierce?' said Bayleaf.

Charisma grinned, glad that his implication had been taken the right way. 'Yeah, you know. So we sort of cohabit for a while, and then if things run smooth, we talk about where we go from there.'

'Marriage?'

Bayleaf's eyes met George's. George, with increasing alarm, said: 'You ain't slung one up it, have you?'

Charisma laughed a man-of-the-world laugh, drained his glass abruptly, and waved knowingly as he headed for the door.

Josie stared at the others. 'All right, what was all that about?'

'You don't know her,' said Bayleaf gloomily. 'She was before your time.'

'Come on. Everybody else seems to be in on it.'

Tony said: 'If that tart's moved in with him . . .' He let it trail away, incapable of predicting the full terrors of the future.

'She's known as the Martini girl,' Malcolm contributed. 'Any time, any place, anywhere.'

'When she moved in with Liver Salts,' said George, 'she didn't have a job or anything. But she didn't half put it about.'

'It gutted him,' Bayleaf recalled. 'He must have lost a good three stone.'

It was all coming back. How Liver Salts had tried to get Donna to leave, but she wouldn't be shifted. How her sharpo little mind had found out all about her rights as a Common Law wife, and how she had taken him through the courts. Only it was more a matter of taking him to the cleaners. She got half of everything he owned. It might not have been any great fortune, but the blow to his pride was a hefty one.

'I imagine that had a lot to do with him applying for a transfer,' said Malcolm.

Josie looked from one to the other. 'You think she might be on the same con with Charisma?'

'Why else is she with him?'

'Perhaps he knows all about her?' said Josie, hoping for the best.

The answer came in unison from all of them. 'No!'

They finished their drinks in a sombre mood. Malcolm was the first to leave. When Josie got up to go, Bayleaf went out with her. Let George and Tony start talking about the two of them if they wanted to; the truth would never be as wretched as the truth about Charisma's half-witted involvements.

They strolled aimlessly along the pavement. There

really was not very much that was safe to say. At last Bayleaf tried something non-committal. 'Got any plans for your day off tomorrow?'

Josie let out a sad little laugh. 'Shades of Liver Salts and Donna. I've had a letter from Gerry's solicitor, saying he wants half of everything. Half of the flat, half of everything in it. So now I'll have to see a solicitor myself, first thing tomorrow.'

'In an ideal world you and Gerry ought to be able to sit down, talk things through, and come to some sort of arrangement.'

And I'm a fine one to talk, he thought ironically.

'In an ideal world,' she echoed. They had gone a few more paces when she said: 'And what about you – your day off?'

'Going down to Folkestone to see Karen.'

'Is she coming back, or what?'

Bayleaf wished he knew the answer to that one. In the clutches of her mother, there was no telling which way Karen would react or what she would be allowed even to think. When they had spoken on the phone, that faraway voice of hers had said in a thin monotone that the doctor had changed her pills and she was doing all right, but she needed time to think. In these last weeks he'd have thought she'd had plenty of time for that.

They reached the corner of the street. Josie hesitated, then kissed him unexpectedly on the cheek and walked briskly away. He loved the way she walked. Not silly sexy, twitching her bottom, or swaying at the hips, but very steadily and gracefully – and very determined, making it clear that she was still her own true self and to hell with whatever fate threw at her.

'Hey!' he called as she stopped, waiting to cross the road. When she turned he raised his voice further, to the alarm of an elderly man plodding past. 'Don't let the buggers grind you down.'

'Nor you, either.' She blew him another kiss. 'Hear me?'

He tried to dismiss her from his thoughts as he drove down to Folkestone the following morning. He wanted to bring Karen back into the forefront of his mind; concentrate on her, bring the whole thing to life again for both of them, the way it ought to be.

When they came face to face again, he knew there was a long way to go. Mrs Grove had let him in, but looked as though she would have been happier to shut the door in his face. She made him wait in the spotless and lifeless sitting-room, as tidy and four-square as all the things she had instilled in her daughter. When she went grudgingly to fetch Karen, Bayleaf felt that he had better remain standing in the window, looking down the street, rather than dare to sit on the sofa with its lace antimacassars or on any of the chairs with their embroidered seats.

Karen came in timidly through the door. Mrs Grove stationed herself immediately behind her. Her eyebrows and tightly clamped lips always seemed to accuse Bayleaf of being some sort of wife-beater.

Karen would be thirty-five next birthday, only a fortnight from now, but in these last few weeks she had acquired the appearance of a rather elderly little girl. It looked as if her mother had done her hair, brushing it and dragging it back with a slide.

'Hello, Mike.' It was little more than a whisper.

He moved towards her and tried to kiss her, but she moved away and slumped into a corner of the sofa, rubbing her neck as if suspicious of anything he might say or do. Mrs Grove did not take her eyes off her son-in-law.

He tried to make it cheery. 'Any chance of a cup of tea?'

For a moment or two he thought Mrs Grove would refuse to budge. Then she moved slowly away, looking

134

back in dark warning. 'I'll be in the kitchen me,' she said to Karen. 'Just shout if you want me.'

When she had gone, Bayleaf tried to grin and shrug it off. Karen squeezed herself further back into the sofa. He had had enough of this. He went to sit beside her, reaching out to put his arm round her. Immediately she was on her feet again, stumbling away.

'I don't want to come back, Mike. Not yet.'

That was not what he had come all these miles to hear, but he made himself get up casually and nod, and keep his voice level and sympathetic. 'No, no. You take as long as you like.' He took his wallet from his inside pocket and pulled out a few notes.

She did not even want to take them from his hand. 'You'd better give those to my Mum.'

He laid the notes on the mantelpiece, even if they did look untidy between the mathematically balanced candlesticks and the two identically framed photographs of Mrs Grove and her late husband. 'There's a bit extra there for a new coat for Melanie. The other one looked a bit short in the sleeves last time I saw her.' He waited for her to respond somehow to that. When she continued standing like an awkward adolescent in the middle of the room, her eyes lowered in contemplation of her shoes, he said: 'If you felt like it later we could pick her up from school. Perhaps get a bite of tea out.'

'Mum always picks her up.'

Bayleaf looked desperately around the room. 'Well' – he could not hold it in – 'it does give her something to do, you two being here. I mean, what would she do if you weren't here – once she'd dusted round, you know.'

Karen lifted her head. She stared at him, her face blank. 'I can't help it, Mike.' When he tried to grab her and hold her, she was as stiff and unyielding as a board.

When Mrs Grove brought the tea tray in, neat with lace doilies, she glanced once at her daughter and glared again at Bayleaf. She made it clear that she would not welcome his company when she went to fetch Melanie from school, but he was not going to let her get away with that. He insisted on accompanying her, hoping Karen would thaw and come with them just to make it a bit easier. Karen disappeared upstairs when the time came and he found himself walking silently beside Mrs Grove.

Kids erupted across the playground. He tried to pick Melanie out from the scurrying figures, but she spotted him first. All at once she was racing towards the railings, and out through the gate into his arms.

'Dad!'

She was hugging him, almost throttling him. A model of a dragon made out of eggboxes was crushed against his shoulder.

'How's my girl?'

'Am I coming home with you? Dad, are we going home?' He felt tears in his eyes, and had a job controlling them when she turned her head to look pleadingly at him. He could not find words; and she recognized what that silence meant. 'Dad, I want to come home with you.' Now she was the one who was sobbing, not trying to hide it.

He had to drag her arms from round his neck before he could put her down. She looked past him at Mrs Grove's implacable face.

Bayleaf took her hand and squeezed it. 'Mel. Listen, Melanie. Dad's got to get back to work soon.'

Her hand slid away from his. She walked towards her grandmother, who put a protective arm round her and stared icily over her head at Bayleaf.

'You see, it only upsets them.'

On the way back through the East End's evening traffic, Bayleaf found himself thinking treacherously again of Josie Ingham. What the hell else was worth thinking about?

10

ANOTHER MORNING, another Watch to face. One by one they were stirring, turning over to snatch one more minute of warmth or reluctantly lurching out of bed towards the bathroom.

Sidney Tate looked across the breakfast table at his wife.

'What would you say if I said I'd had it?'

Nancy contemplated him with her cup of tea in mid-air. 'I'd say "who with?", because you haven't had it with me for ages.'

He wasn't in the mood for that sort of crack. This was serious; deadly serious. 'I mean the job. I'm up to here with the job.' He dared not put it more strongly than that. He would have hated to tell anyone, even Nancy – maybe Nancy least of all – how he had started dreading the bells going down. His heart would race. His mouth went dry. He got hot and cold sweats; but he dared not let any of the men even guess it. 'I've been thinking seriously,' he went on, 'about getting out. Find myself something else while I'm still young enough.'

'What – pushing fifty, and when you've spent your whole life in uniform?'

'There's always openings for mature men of discipline and experience.'

'Where? Cinema or theatre usherette? Or geared up in one of those long coats and a top hat with a cockade on it, opening car doors outside the Ritz? Come off it, Sidney, you're just a bit cheesed off, that's all.'

He might have known there was no way of getting through to her. She didn't live the job every hour of the Watch and have nightmares about it afterwards – and nowadays have them even before he set out. So far as she was concerned, he left the house at certain times and got back at rather uncertain times. It wasn't fair to expect her to want to know any more.

He got up to go. At the door she caught up with him, kissed him on the cheek and patted him on the shoulder. 'It'll pass, Sidney. It's only the menopause.'

At the same time Charisma, running late, was forcing himself away from Donna's warm, moist body, doing without breakfast rather than sacrifice a last few minutes of her clinging, ecstatic movements. Oh, this was the real thing all right . . .

Meanwhile Tony Sanderson was digging under the kitchen sink for a plastic bag. He crammed his gear into it and looked at Dorothy's smooth white neck above the blue of her dressing-gown, then kissed it. She put her teacup down and turned to put her arms round him for a moment.

'So,' he said, 'what you planning to do while I'm on watch?'

'What d'you mean, what am I planning to do? What do I usually do?'

'I don't know. I thought you might be going out or something.'

She flinched. 'Tony, if I was going out I'd say I was going out, wouldn't I?' When he did not reply she got up and put her cheek against his. 'Suddenly you don't believe me any more. Look, I told you there was nothing in that business the other night. Jenny and I came out of the pub, and . . . oh, look, I've told you already. I wouldn't cheat on you, darling, honest. I don't want you going out on watch with doubts about me. I couldn't bear it if anything happened to you.'

140

Marion Cartwright, also still in her dressing-gown, looked pale and frowsy as she sipped her tea. Morning sickness had begun a couple of days ago and she was not enjoying it. Nor was she enjoying her husband's blatant preoccupation with his own worries rather than with hers.

'If anyone comes,' he urged, 'I'm not here, all right?'

'You're never here.'

'No, all right, but listen. If anyone comes I'm not here and you don't know where I am or when I'm likely to be home, right?'

'I never do know where you are,' she said acidly, 'or when you'll be home.' As he gave up and turned towards the door, curiosity stirred in her at last. 'Look, what's going on? When you say anyone . . .?'

'Anyone. Especially a bloke with a roofing hammer. All right?'

He left the house slowly, checking both ways before venturing out into the street. Of course he ought to have spent his last free day finishing off that garage job for Eddie instead of nipping round to the Italian woman again. He admitted that now, though only to himself. But time had gone by and then it had been too late to show up and get anything worthwhile done. It hadn't seemed to matter much at the time, but now it was beginning to get a bit heavy. In his bones he knew that Eddie would sooner or later come looking for him. And he wasn't too optimistic about the state of his bones when Big Eddie had finished.

So the members of Blue Watch drove, walked, cycled or took the bus to reach Blackwall Fire Station and assemble for parade in the Appliance room. Another Watch, another long stretch of hours out of your life, another period of boredom or bitchery or violent action.

* * *

The arrival of Liver Salts ensured that boredom gave way to speculation and the anticipation of an explosion – not in some chemical factory or gas main, but right here on the premises.

Bayleaf had been dishing out sausage, mash and peas from the serving hatch when the phone rang. Malcolm, the closest, picked it up and said: 'Monkey House.' Then he waved the receiver at Josie. 'For you-oo-oo.'

Bayleaf stopped slapping his serving spoon noisily against plates, and looked anxiously at Josie. Gerry again? The rest of them pretended not to listen, but it was a pretty poor effort.

She had indeed half expected to hear Gerry's voice, complaining or threatening something. It turned out to be quite different; smoother and more languid than Gerry, quietly confident where Gerry was either cringing or cocky. For a moment she did not recognize the speaker, and wondered at his assumption that she would. Then he said: 'David.' She fitted the voice to the face – across the classroom to a background of slow, laborious Spanish, and across the table when they had had coffee together. Josie could almost visualize the odd lift of his right eyebrow as he spoke. As she wondered how he had tracked down the number of her particular station, he was saying: 'I thought of suggesting a drink and a bite to eat after class tomorrow.'

'Well, I . . . I don't know.'

'Didn't want to spring it on you at short notice. Thought I'd give you time to prepare yourself.'

What did he mean by that? Expecting her to smarten herself up, be ready for a whirl, staying out late?

'Just a drink,' she said.

There was the faintest hesitation, then there was a chuckle in his voice. 'Just a drink.'

'Well, maybe. We'll see how we feel after the class.'

There were murmurs and whistles as soon as she put

the phone down. Bayleaf, framed in the serving hatch, resumed his banging of spoon and plates. She risked a timid smile as he passed her food across to her, and he forced a wry response.

'Permission to come aboard?'

A brawny, well set-up man stood in the doorway. With his wide face and very wide grin he looked larger than lifesize. Malcolm and Tony got up, shouting a welcome and slapping him on the back, urging him into the room. Josie watched curiously. Nobody bothered to introduce her to the stranger, who was obviously not a stranger to the rest of them.

Bayleaf came out from the kitchen. 'Liver Salts! How're you getting on, old son?'

It was boisterous and clumsily boyish. Josie sat back and watched, and was the first to see Charisma coming into the mess. As he spotted Liver Salts he came to a dead halt, then forced himself to go to the table and sit down.

Liver Salts must already have heard rumours. He spoke very carefully. 'How's it going, Charisma?'

'Terrific.' Charisma stared fixedly down at the table. 'But what's it got to do with you?'

There was an uneasy silence. It was broken by Sicknote crashing in, unusually cheerful and with no imminent sign of physical injury to justify his leaving the premises. Maybe he was saving it all up for a complaint against the standard of Bayleaf's grub, destined to give him food poisoning.

At the sight of Liver Salts he began singing cheerily, 'Any time, any place, anywhere.' He punched Liver Salts just above the elbow. 'Things on the up and up, eh? Finished paying off the horrible costs of experience? Could have told you all along that you'd got yourself a right slag with that one. I know a nasty affliction when I see one.'

'Sicknote . . .'

'You're well shot of her. Cured, eh? Looking ten times healthier. I hear she ran you through some sticky patches, though. Hey, George, what was that they called him at Kilburn afterwards?'

'Sicknote,' said Liver Salts ominously.

But Sicknote was almost wetting himself with mirth. 'Numb Nuts, wasn't it? Also known as Donna's Disease.'

Charisma's face had gone bright red. He pushed himself up and slammed his fist down on the table. Josie prayed there wasn't going to be a row. Mickey-taking was everyday rations in here, but really personal nastiness could mean trouble in the team. And a team that ceased to be a team was the ultimate trouble.

'She told me all about him.' Charisma stabbed a trembling finger at Liver Salts. 'All the time she was with him, he was knocking off another bird.'

'Now wait a minute, mate – '

'And he promised he was going to marry her, but he never did.'

'This is a load of crap,' raged Liver Salts. 'Do you know how much lucre she bled off me? Have you any idea – '

'All of it hers by rights,' Charisma yelled back. 'And if you want to know what sort of girl Donna really is, she give all that to her sister to put a deposit on a starter home. And you know the thanks she got for it? Her sister's husband trying to get his leg over.'

Liver Salts looked at the spellbound audience and spread his hands helplessly. 'She's spinning him the same line. Same line as when I first met her.' He turned fiercely on Charisma. 'You want to watch yourself, or she's going to make you look a right wanker. And not just here, but right through the Brigade.'

Charisma was still trembling, but he was not going

144

to turn away. 'I love her, and I trust her. She told me you'd slag her off if I ever saw you. Now me and Donna are all right. Get it? I don't need your advice or anybody else's. And you lot can keep your snouts out. I can look after myself. There's no flies on me.'

As he stormed out they all began a loud buzzing sound which followed him a few steps along the corridor. Without warning he turned and came back into the room, heading straight for Liver Salts. Liver Salts was bigger and tougher and looked like what he was – an ex-Marine – but Charisma's surprise attack threw him backwards against a chair, and he went down with a crash on to the floor. As he struggled up ready to hit back with everything he'd got, Bayleaf threw himself between them.

Then the bells went down.

Josie dashed thankfully away from the table. Whatever the crisis this time, it could hardly generate much more heat than what had been threatening to frazzle the air in the mess.

George Green was first on to the pump, still buzzing like an energetic bluebottle as Charisma slid down the pole and raced towards him.

'Just keep that up, George,' Bayleaf warned, 'and you're liable to arrive at this shout with your face where your arse used to be.'

George scrambled aboard. 'Does that mean I'll have to wear me helmet on me bum for the rest of me life?' He held out his hand to help Charisma up. It was ignored.

The place was well alight by the time they arrived. It was a line of lock-ups with lopsided doors and a forecourt of cracked concrete sprouting some ambitious weeds. The call had been for the Watch to deal with an outbreak of fire from a heap of rubbish inside. Tate took one look and announced that this was no run-of-the-mill rubbish job. The smoke pouring out from the top of one door was not the smoke of some garden bonfire but contained thick and oily fumes, stinking of something he could believe might be lethal.

'Bayleaf.'

'Guv?'

'Request normal attendance.'

Malcolm Cross and George Green were making hoses. It was only when Tate let out a mighty bellow that they looked round to see Charisma heading full tilt towards the lock-up with his axe.

'You stupid sod, what d'you think – '

'Back,' Tate was yelling. 'Get right back!' He looked round at the inevitable crowd of onlookers. It was always the same. You felt in the end that even the faces were all the same, drawn from a pool of permanent nosy-parkers available for appearances anywhere at the drop of a hat. 'Does anybody know what's gone up in there?'

Nobody was going to volunteer any information – which did not mean that none of them knew. Somebody had raised the alarm, and that same somebody could have known why a 999 fire brigade call had become a matter of urgency. But that was the sort of question you got round to asking after you had brought the smoke and smouldering flames under control.

Too late, the station officer saw that Fireman Appleby was either disobeying orders or had not heard them. Charisma had gone for the right-hand door of the end lock-up like a bull at a gate, crouching and jabbing at it with his axe. He was bracing himself for a final onslaught when the door began sagging slowly outwards. Charisma reached out with his free hand as if to tear it bodily from its hinges. Suddenly he was surrounded by a halo of white heat. The door exploded outwards, flinging him a good five yards across the concrete in front of the lock-ups. Flame showered down on him and began rising up from his hands as if he were offering up a fierce votive candle in some leftover of a pagan ceremony.

At the same time he was screaming.

Bayleaf crouched and ran towards him, keeping his head well down below the swirling fumes.

'Get those lines in there,' Tate was shouting. George and Malcom were making a V with the hoses to clear a way for Bayleaf to get close to Charisma and get enough grip to pull him out. 'And get an ambulance.' Tate sounded close to hysteria. It was not like him. Something was going to crack soon.

Bayleaf wrestled Charisma back from the blaze. Inside the lock-up there was a succession of popping noises as drums of chemicals gave out their dragon's breath to fuel the conflagration. Malcolm and George began to scramble into their chemical protection suits and breathing apparatus as the pump ladder team came howling on to the scene.

'What happened?' Josie shielded her eyes against the ferocious glare.

'Charisma's copped it,' said Bayleaf bluntly.

'He was poxed off with me.' George sounded guilty as he vanished into the camouflage of his C.P.S.

Bayleaf glared at Sicknote. 'He was poxed off with all of us, poor sod.'

There was suddenly a second, larger explosion. An eerie cloud of yellow vapour started curling out to engulf them, snaking and swirling with an evil life of its own. Those standing well back on the outskirts, who were without breathing apparatus, began to cough. Until now there had been no obvious breeze, but all at once a wind had sprung up and was gleefully spreading the poisonous cloud into the warren of streets nearby. Beneath the feet of the men edging closer to the seat of the eruption there was a hissing and bubbling as if some alien force was determined to gobble up their feet and then work its way upwards.

Josie sipped her tea at the mess table and wiped the back of her hand wearily across her brow. It came away grimy with a dark souvenir of the fire. She shuddered to think what her face must look like but was too exhausted to stagger along to the washroom and check on it.

Station Officer Tate came in and surveyed them all. He looked more depressed than they had ever seen him. They had been through worse battles than this one, but they had never lost a man before. This time it looked as if their fortunes had changed; and Tate was in no mood for bad luck of this kind.

'I'm just going to get on to the blower to the hospital. Find out how Charisma is.' Despondently he added, 'Anyone any idea who his next of kin would be now his Mum's gone? There's nobody listed on his card.'

Sicknote gulped. 'I didn't know his Mum had gone.'

Bayleaf put his head in his hands. 'Well, he never had a Dad. His Mum was his Nan, sort of thing. His real Mum he called his sister – emigrated when he was a kid. He didn't say where.'

'When d'you hear all this?'

Bayleaf looked up, blinking. He was so tired and choked up that he had hardly realized how much he was giving away. 'He asked me not to tell the lads,' he recalled.

'And you never did, did you?' said Tate sardonically as he left the room.

Josie reached out a sympathetic hand. 'So it just leaves the Martini girl?'

'Yeah,' said Bayleaf. 'Just the Martini girl.'

Josie washed her face at the end of the Watch and made her way to the hospital. Somebody had to go and check up. Tate had come back to report that Charisma, incredibly, was still alive. But only just. He had been in surgery, where they had had to cut his gloves away very carefully before they could start anything else, and they were not all that sanguine about his chances. Josie felt that in their minds the men had fatalistically written Charisma off. He did seem to have chucked himself almost deliberately into that danger. But she was not going to be as pessimistic as the rest of them.

As she waited in a corridor outside the ward, a girl with red painted lips and suspicious eyes, twitching from side to side, came mincing towards her, jangling with earrings and a charm bracelet.

She looked and sounded peevish. 'Ain't there no doctor or sister around anywhere?'

Josie had been wondering this herself, but assumed that somehow it was like the duty watches at the station: one shift went off and another came on, and there was a lull while they swapped notes. She said: 'You got someone in here?'

The girl nodded, still fidgeting and looking around, her fingers never still and her head pecking and probing.

'Me too,' said Josie, making conversation. 'I've got a mate here somewhere. A fireman.'

'Fireman Appleby?'

Of course. The descriptions offered by those of Blue Watch who had known her left little doubt. 'You're not Donna?'

'Yeah.'

'I'm Josie Ingham. In the same crowd as Chari . . . Leslie. Do you know how he is?'

Donna avoided her eyes. 'I just got this call saying he was in here,' she said petulantly. 'They said he got burned. Badly.'

'I know. I was there. I thought I'd look in before I went home.'

Donna was still fidgeting, trying to work out how all

this added up. 'I hope he's not so bad he can't work again, or he's been really badly disfigured, like.'

'If he has, he'll need someone to stand by him.'

Donna looked desperately around, anywhere but at Josie. 'Well, the thing is I hardly know him.'

No, thought Josie. And she didn't suppose Charisma really knew Donna, either.

Donna crept unhappily down the ward to the bed with the drawn curtains indicated by the nurse. She looked back once, then peered inside and edged towards the bed.

'Hello, Leslie. Leslie . . .?'

His hands were bandaged. The hair above his forehead was singed, and there were burn marks like a rash all down his face. Ointment glistened on his cheeks and under his chin. His eyes were closed, and as she reached the side of the bed he winced. Then his scorched, blackened lips began to move. It was difficult to tell whether he was moaning in pain or trying to say something.

She put her head close to his. 'What, Leslie?'

Faintly he began to sing. 'Any time, any place, anywhere.'

Donna straightened up. Her careful whisper became a yell of fury. 'I knew it, I knew it! That Liver Salts has been slagging me off, ain't he?'

An outraged nurse pulled the curtain back and stormed in.

11

BLUE WATCH had ended an uneventful night and were eating bacon sandwiches washed down with tea when Oliver Parish of Red Watch came into the mess with a rolled-up poster under his arm. He crossed the room to the noticeboard and groaned.

'Typical. Only two drawing pins. We've got a theory in Red Watch that you lot eat 'em like sweets, just like you do with all the bog paper.' He prised the pins from an out-of-date notice and began putting the new one up.

Bayleaf watched from the far side of the table. 'Another of your dead-or-alive posters, Jaffa? Anyone who's not actually buried and still has four limbs and two eyes and a nose is wanted for use as a punchbag by the L.F.S. Boxing Club, right?'

'Why do they call him Jaffa?' asked young Kevin artlessly.

Bayleaf lowered his voice. 'Because he's seedless, that's why. Had the same op as the cat.'

All of them except George Green began drifting round the table to inspect the notice. It announced the South West Area Charity Boxing Challenge. A middleweight from South West Area was throwing down the gauntlet to any middleweights from the other four areas who fancied they could go ten rounds with him in the ring. Before meeting him they would have to meet each other, and the winner would then meet the challenger.

'Conker Coburn they call him,' Jaffa announced.

George winced silently. He knew all about young Coburn, or as much as anyone in his right mind would want to know. In any case he wanted to keep a low profile on things like that. He had hung up his gloves six years ago and hoped that everyone else had forgotten all about that part of his career.

Malcolm was skimming over the details. 'So who are we entering from our area?'

'That's the problem,' said Jaffa. 'We can't lay our hands on anybody. The middleweight who might have represented us has flitted off to join the New York Fire Department. Cleaned us out of our best boxers they did, the bastards.'

'But this is outrageous,' said Malcolm in his most haughty manner. 'As a matter of honour, our area simply can't *not* compete.'

He looked from one face to another. They all began looking at one another, ruling Josie out for a start but debating who else might be suitable. George finished his sandwich and made a point of catching nobody's eye.

Matters came to a head in the Locker room. Hanging his gear up, young Kevin, a probationer but one who was beginning to throw his weight about, nodded bossily at George. Vaseline stared and nodded. The others began to cluster round.

'A natural, of course,' said Malcolm. 'That nose – we should have remembered.'

'Oh, no.' George shrugged his jacket on. 'You can knock that one on the head, fellers. I ain't going in for any boxing competition.'

'I think you're wrong about that, old chap.'

'Forget it. Haven't had a serious dig at anyone for years. And I ain't fit.'

'Then get fit.'

George fumed. According to that poster, it was two weeks before the first bout. He would need months of training and dieting to get anywhere near fitness. And he was willing to bet none of them had ever seen Conker Coburn or heard anything about him. George might not have kept his fists up, but he still kept an interest in who was up-and-coming and who had gone down with a thump. He knew that Coburn was nineteen years of age, built like a brick toilet block, with a right punch on him like a steam hammer. It was said he was so fast that the only time you could actually see him was when he was fast asleep. George on the other hand was twenty-seven years of age, had not trained or had a pair of gloves on in years, and he was not going to give Conker Coburn the chance to wipe the floor with him.

'You're out of your boxes, the lot of you,' he said with heavy finality, and went out across the yard, closely followed by Vaseline.

For a moment, still with thoughts of the boxing ring in his head, he thought he was being accosted by a heavyweight in the mood for mayhem. A man with massive shoulders and fists like hams was blocking the way to his car, hunched in a menacing effect which was only slightly spoilt by his greasy woolly bonnet.

'Do you know a Roland round here?' The tone of voice was well in line with his appearance.

'Roland?' The name rang no bells with George. 'Never heard of him, mate.'

Malcolm and Sicknote came sauntering across the yard. Vaseline had somehow disappeared – maybe gone back indoors to fetch something he had forgotten.

'Look' – the tone was growing uglier – 'this Roland stitched me up for a ton, right? I know he's a fire-man, and I hear on the grapevine this is where he hangs out.'

'Well, I don't want to blind you with science, old chap,' drawled Malcolm, 'but there are four Watches at every station: Red, White, Green and Blue. Now, this character's not in Blue Watch, because that's us. And he's not in Red because they've just come on and we know them pretty well. So maybe this Roland, whoever he is, is in Green or White, so maybe you should call back and ask again when they're on?'

The man's shoulders hunched. His deeply sunken eyes ranged suspiciously from one face to the next. 'Why do I get the feeling that you bunch are trying to take me for a ride?'

They all looked shocked, and at last he turned and stumped off into the street. Malcolm followed but turned in the opposite direction. Sicknote detached his bike from the railings and set off. George Green was about to get into his car when Vaseline groped his way upright on the far side. 'Is it all right? He's gone?'

'Wondered where you'd got to. Come to think of it, you're a Roland, aren't you? What was all that about?'

'Nice bloke, isn't he?' Vaseline was still trembling. 'As soon as I've got the money together I'll pay him off. It'll be all right.'

George opened the car door. He didn't want to know the details. Vaseline ought to be greasy enough to slide out of his own scrapes by now.

'Look, George.' Vaseline held on to the edge of the door. 'Please, mate, I could do with somewhere to stay.'

'Don't tell me you haven't got a home to go to any longer.'

'I just meant for a night or two. Somewhere he won't find me. I mean, you could see for yourself. If big Eddie catches up with me, I'm a classic case of death.'

'You don't mean the geezer's going to top you just because you owe him a ton?'

'You don't know him, mate,' breathed Vaseline. 'He's done time for GBH. A nutter. He used to be a meat cutter at Smithfield. Amputated his own brother's ears just because he broke the wing mirrors on his van.'

It was no good waving Vaseline away and telling him to get on with it. Your mates might be nutcases in a dozen different ways and a downright pain in the arse on some boring watches; but they were mates, and you couldn't toss them to the wolves. Or, in this case, to something with all the dimensions and power of a grizzly bear.

He leaned over to push the other door open.

'Just one thing. If you're staying at my place, where's Marion staying?'

'I dunno. Maybe she'll stay with her Dad.'

'But what if she don't stay round her Dad's?' George reasoned patiently. 'What if she stays at your place and that roofer slips round there and smashes it up? I mean, she's pregnant.'

'Not my fault.'

George stared. 'What d'you mean? Marion made medical history? Wasn't you who made here pregnant – just some virus?'

Vaseline grinned feebly but not longer had the strength to summon up any further excuses.

Josie had heaved the bag of dry cleaning and her shopping out of the Metro and was trying not to drop them while she fumbled for her key, when she saw a familiar figure getting out of a cab on the far side of the road. She had opened the front door and was in the hallway when he reached her.

She remembered the flashy paintwork and the logo. 'What happened to the motor?'

'Lost the sales job,' said Gerry. 'Lost the company car.' He shrugged as if this was all in the day's work, or loss of work, which for him it was. Lost jobs were the story of his life. 'And now,' he said insinuatingly, 'lost wife, lost home too.'

Without waiting for an invitation he followed her along the narrow cream-coloured hall to the kitchen. While she pushed the dry cleaning into a corner and began to empty her shopping bag he prowled around, inspecting everything as if to make a choice of what he would take away with him. He came to a halt at the table, where she had left the folder of the Leading Fireman's/Firewoman's Course. There were also brochures for a Spanish holiday.

'Going off for a fortnight – with Bayleaf, maybe?'

'Yes,' said Josie tensely. 'Me and Bayleaf and the whole of Blue Watch. We're hiring a small jet, but we'll all muck in and share the one hotel bedroom, of course.'

He resumed his ambling. She followed him into the sitting-room, determined not to let him out of her sight. He paused by the stereo and stooped to take a few records out of their slots below it. She had guessed that he would want to take the record-player and those records, which he had somehow always regarded as particularly his own rather than part of their shared life.

He put half a dozen on one side, paused, and added an LP of The Police. She remembered buying him that one as part of a Christmas present along with some expensive leather gloves. And it all came back. He had lost one of the gloves the evening they went to see *Jaws*. She almost wanted to make a joke of it and tell him it was probably still under the seat where he had hidden – and remind him that it was the same night that he had got food poisoning from a prawn curry.

Gerry studied a surrealist picture on a record-sleeve. 'Happy days,' he said.

'Some of them were very happy,' she said gently. And studying his downcast gaze, the sadness of his whole stance – even though it was a familiar, so often overdone way of standing and brooding – she had to go on. 'Gerry, I haven't said this before. Maybe now's as good a time as any. I mean, I hope we're not going to go on being bitter with each other. I don't want to hold any grudges. I hope you won't, either.'

But his eyes when at last he looked up were clouded with resentment and self-pity.

'It'd help if I could borrow the car.'

'If you could *what*?'

'There's a chance of a rep's job in Portsmouth. And maybe something in Croydon. But I do need to whizz about a bit for a few days. It would simplify things – save on the train fares – there's nothing like being mobile, you know.' When she hesitated he said: 'And how else am I to get the record-player and the discs back to my slum?'

Oh, she knew. She also knew that she was a mug. Who was to say that she would ever get the car back? But she was the one who had said there ought to be no bitterness. This was not the time to say that he wasn't to be relied upon, and that she couldn't see why she should lift a finger to help him.

'Just a few days?' she said.

'Just a few days.'

The idea of going out to a cinema and then having something to eat was something which had not crossed John Hallam's mind for a long time. You did that sort of thing when you were courting, of course, but once the courting was over and the marriage began, there was a mortgage and the cost of running the house and then the kids and then everything else. Hiring a baby-sitter cost money on top of what it cost you to go out; and you couldn't be too sure how reliable the girl was likely to be. So you kept putting it off; and the wife grew more and more crotchety; and you got crosser and crosser because she failed to understand what the demands of the job were like, and how little chance there was of getting promotion or a salary increase or any damned thing to make life easier. Going to the pictures? There was the telly – always the telly – and something simple to eat in front of it.

Now old Albert had come up with the notion. He was on the premises, he'd got nothing to do, the kids would be all right with him. And while they were at it, why didn't John take Sandra out for a nice meal somewhere afterwards?

'She don't get out enough,' Albert wheezed, one eye still on the snooker table dominating the television screen. 'I'm always saying that.'

And Sandra, thought Hallam ruefully, was always saying that, too. So it was the pictures and probably a meal afterwards. Casting a critical gaze on Albert's rheumy eyes, he wondered if the old swine was capable of staying awake that long, or hearing a sound if either of the kids did set up a wail. But the offer had been made, and you might as well take advantage of him while he was on the premises. Better than sitting in with him every evening and listening to the drivelling crap he talked, or watching the deadly programmes he insisted on.

'You're all right, then?' Hallan tried to make it sound bluff and friendly.

Albert for once looked remarkably contented.

The film was no great shakes, but there were some torrid lovemaking scenes which made Sandra reach out and grasp his hand and nuzzle up against his shoulder, just the way she used to do when their bodies were strange and untried together. And at least there was an extra something about the wide screen and the loud sound-track which you didn't get from the telly in the corner of the sitting-room.

He put his arm round her. She was warm and cuddly and smiling, and across the table in the Chinese restaurant she went on smiling, and he knew why he had married her. He could only pray that scruffy old Albert, who had made this possible, wouldn't find some way of ruining it when they got home. He would never understand how Sandra had come to have such a grotty delinquent of a father.

There was silence when they let themselves into the house shortly after midnight. Presumably Albert had shuffled off to bed. Hallam could only hope that he had left his bedroom door open as instructed, and was not too far gone to hear the kids if they woke up.

Sandra went into the sitting-room and switched on the light.

Albert blinked into the glare and disentangled himself from the arms of a plump, elderly lady who occupied more than her fair share of the sofa. His daughter let out a little splutter, backed away, and closed the door.

Hallam said: 'I don't believe it.'

Sandra giggled. 'Life in the old dog yet!'

'But who could ever find the insanitary old – '

'I've had a lovely evening,' said Sandra firmly. 'Don't go and spoil it.'

'First the flowers. Now the forbidden fruit. The dirty old codger.'

'I'm sure they wouldn't have . . . well, at their age, I mean . . .' Sandra was caught between incredulous laughter and revulsion. 'I'll make a pot of tea.' It was her remedy for all major problems. 'Then we can all go to bed.'

'I'm not having that old woman staying here in my house and going to bed with – '

'Don't be ridiculous.' Sandra went to put the electric kettle on.

They were neither of them quite sure how ridiculous it really was.

When Sandra carried the tea tray in, the two were sitting on the sofa looking like a couple of gauche teenagers. Sandra did a lot of unnecessary bustling about, putting on a big act with the teacups and the pot, handing things to the visitor and waiting for her father to make some excuse, or comment, or at least a proper introduction. In the end, getting no joy in that direction, she said pointedly:

'It's nice to know that Dad has some nice company, Miss . . . Mrs . . .?'

'Call me Edith.'

'Edith. You live nearby?'

Edith, it transpired, was seventy-four years of age and had been living at the old folks' home on the edge of the park for the last five years. Although she did not go into detail, there was a hint that she liked to go for a stroll in the park every afternoon, and this was where Albert had picked her up. Not that either of them would have used such a coarse phrase.

Sandra was effusive and very attentive. She poured a second cup of tea, glanced at her husband as if to make it clear that the romantic mood of the cinema and the meal for two required some fulfilment fairly soon, and said: 'Won't Matron be worried about you being out so late?'

Hallam sighed. The old bat had said seventy-four, not fourteen. He wondered if old Albert was going to offer gallantly to walk her back to the home. It was bitterly cold out, but Albert's senile ardour would probably keep the blood circulating briskly enough. And when he shambled back, would he be whistling or mumbling some stupid song the way he so often did, without rhyme

160

or reason? Only this time there did seem to be a reason, however improbable.

Hallam studied his own sofa with distaste. There had been some moments to remember on that sofa, a while back. He was not sure he liked it being misused by two senile delinquents like this. Maybe the old folks' home would find accommodation for Albert. That sort of behaviour ought to keep the place swinging until the small hours of the morning.

Sandra looked at him suggestively; then, recognizing his withdrawn expression, became agitated and impatient.

The chill of the evening made Josie curse herself for letting Gerry con her out of the car so easily. She had trailed along on the bus to her night class, and went without much enthusiasm under the pallidly lit windows to the drab entrance. The only consolation was that she reached the door just as a fine drizzle began to blow across the playground. It seemed a wildly unsuitable place in which to learn the warm, lilting language of sunny Spain.

She had been unsure about the idea of having drinks with David, but after struggling through an evening's exercises to the accompaniment of rain swishing against the window, she was glad of a kindred spirit to talk to.

'One thing, though,' she said as they left the building and prepared to sprint to the pub on the corner. 'One condition if we do have a drink. I buy my round. That's something I won't argue about.'

He smiled that crooked, sidelong smile of his, half mocking and half deferring to her.

The pub was probably crammed with businessmen every lunchtime. At this hour of the evening it had only a few regulars in one corner and a sombre, solitary man

161

who might have postponed his return home from the office a couple of hours too long.

Choosing a table in the remotest possible corner, David proved to have a disconcerting habit of staring straight into her eyes without blinking. The lopsided smile and the evasive glances suddenly came into direct focus, as if he planned to hypnotize her now that he had the chance. He talked amiably and offhandedly enough about his work as an accountant for a Croydon firm of which she had vaguely heard, making it sound ironically funny rather than dull, with stories of crooked dealers, offshore tax dodgers, and Inland Revenue inspectors in pursuit of the wrong man while the villain was long ago on his way to the Cayman Islands. There was something rather too self-congratulatory about it, though; he smirked every now and then, not at the facts but at his own cleverness. Some of the stories even sounded too neat to be true, as if he had read or heard them somewhere and polished them up for his own purposes.

Josie felt a prickle of unease. She was glad she had promised only to come for a drink. If they had gone out to dinner together the evening would have dragged on and she would have been unable to get away. As it was, she had bought the second lot of drinks, they were quits, and when she had drained her glass she felt she could reasonably leave and go home. She was tired, and found she was ceasing to hear half of what he was saying.

'Well.' She reached for her handbag. 'I'd better be off.'

'Time for another?'

'Thanks, no. Another time.' It was an obvious, polite thing to say, but all at once she wished she hadn't said it.

Outside the wind had come up and sleet was driving

at an angle across the road. Josie turned towards the bus stop, where one woman was waiting under the shelter of a wind-tossed umbrella.

David said: 'Look, I realize you're a very independent girl, and I do respect you for that. But you can't hang about waiting for a bus at this time of night. Not in this weather.' She watched a gang of youths scuffling on the corner by a zebra crossing and heard somebody shouting obscenities over and over again. 'You can't rely on the damned things even during the day,' David was saying. 'I'd be very worried leaving you here to get home on your own.'

'Oh, I'm used to it by now.'

'Don't be silly. Let me run you back.'

She was too weary to argue, and she was getting cold. 'Okay, thanks. That's very kind.'

She gave him directions and sat back with her eyes closed against the confusion of reflected lights on the wet road. Then she opened them again with a start to make sure he didn't take a wrong turning. It seemed an eternity before they drew up at the kerb. She was looking forward to a hot drink and bed.

David reached across her as if to open the door; but his hand settled on hers. 'I don't suppose I get invited in for a cup of coffee?'

Josie snatched her hand away. She might have known.

'All right.' He laughed suddenly. 'If you won't spare my blushes . . . I'm bursting for a pee. Ought to have gone before we left the pub.'

She could not help grinning. 'Why didn't you say?'

'Because I'm a shy suburban accountant, aren't I? I was very carefully brought up not to broadcast my needs.'

'Okay.'

She led the way in. As she was hanging her coat on the hall-stand she waved him towards the door of the loo. Things felt better and warmer indoors. Safe on her own territory, she heard herself say: 'Now you're here, you might as well have that coffee.'

'Ah, the ice maiden melteth. Jolly good.'

She went on into the kitchen and took the jar of instant coffee from the cupboard. As she switched the electric kettle on there was the measured beat of his footsteps coming quietly and steadily into the room behind her.

'When you're being an incredibly brave London firefighting lady, what do you wear?'

'Rubber boots, waterproof leggings, and a very fetching yellow cork helmet.'

'I should imagine a man might learn to find that very sexy.'

Josie spooned coffee granules into two mugs. 'I should imagine a man would be very odd if he did.'

As she turned towards the fridge for the milk, she found he had planted himself in front of her. His voice was lower, with a slight hiss through his teeth. 'You mean to tell me those incredibly brave London firefighting gentlemen don't find you sexy when you're on the job?'

She was beginning to be very sorry she had let him smooth-talk his way in here. 'No,' she said coldly, 'because those incredibly brave London firefighting gentlemen are generally too busy doing their job to think about whether they find me sexy or not.'

When she tried to get past him to the fridge door, he grinned and dodged in front of her. She tried to go the other way, and he began dancing to and fro, with a fixed grin that somehow sent a chill through her.

'Don't do that,' she snapped. 'I don't like it. I don't like blokes who piss about like little boys. I find it tedious.'

His grin became a mock-rueful smile, and he backed

away while she opened the fridge door. As it closed, he lunged forward again and pinned her to the door. She dropped the milk and heard the open carton split on the floor, while her left arm was trapped behind her. His face was angry, and his hands were savage. His groin thrust heavily against her and began working to and fro while he clamped his lips to her mouth and tried to shove his tongue forward. Josie wrestled her head aside but he made a grab for her and bit her lip. His right hand clawed down from her face to her shoulder and then down to her breasts, and his lips abandoned her mouth for an assault on her neck. 'Playing hard to get?' The words and breath rasped against her throat. 'Don't tell me you don't enjoy it.'

She tugged her left hand free and made a grab at that insistent groin of his. He yelped and staggered backwards. Josie reached wildly for the first thing in range. It was the kettle. She wrenched it so that the lead sprang from its socket, and clouted him on the side of the head with it. She was storming forward for a second blow when she slipped in the milk and went down on her back. He pounced at once, grabbing her by the hair and hauling her to her feet. In desperation she tore herself free, leaving a cluster of hairs between his fingers. Before he could get at her again she pulled at the cutlery drawer and clamped her hand round the handle of the carving knife.

'One step nearer and I'll make a soprano out of you, you bastard.'

He rocked to and fro on his heels for a moment. Then he was all smiles again, positively elated, as if this was the highspot of his evening. He gave a deprecatory shrug, and risked a teasing little movement towards her.

'I mean it,' said Josie.

This time he produced a mocking little bow. 'I'm sorry.' He took a few mincing steps backwards, then turned and went out.

Josie waited for the front door to shut. When she heard it slam she tossed the knife on to the work surface, took a shuddering breath, and hurried out. Once the door was locked and the chain was on, she was going to need to clean up and do something about her gashed lip.

She had her hand on the bolt when David erupted suddenly from the loo, where he had been waiting.

His hands were groping for her again. She screamed and tried to heave the front door open. He got his arm round her neck and dragged her backwards. When she collapsed to her knees he leaned down to tug at her skirt, his face leering close to hers. She managed to pull herself half up, and pushed down with all her failing strength on one knee. Her other knee went up between his legs, and this time her aim was perfect. Robbed of breath, he swayed for a moment. It was enough. She opened the flat door with one hand and reached for him with the other, getting a grip on his ear and swinging him out into the passage, rushing him along to the front door and out into the night.

Back in her own hallway, with shaking hands she flipped the catch on the lock, slammed the bolt home, and on the third attempt got the knob of the chain into its slot.

It was half an hour before she felt she could go to bed without tossing and turning and reliving every moment of this foul evening. She took a couple of aspirins and went into the shower to clean away all the contamination. Looking in the mirror, she realized that her cut and bloodied lip was going to cause some

166

comment among Blue Watch tomorrow. One remark about love bites, she thought hysterically, and she might deal with the lot of them the way she had threatened to deal with David.

12

T HE THREE of them were tired after a hard day. There
was good enough reason – three shouts, and one of
those a pretty hairy business – but none of it had been
as tiring as just sitting here at a hospital bedside forcing
out conversation. Charisma's dog-eyed gratitude did not
make it any easier. You felt you had to keep on patting
his head and making affectionate noises, even when you
had run out of ideas.

Malcolm suppressed a yawn. 'So when do you expect
to be out, then?'

'In a few days, with a bit of luck. They've given me
a card to go down Outpatients next week. Ain't the
burns,' said Charisma stoically, 'they're more or less
okay now. It's the head injury. I suppose they're worried
there might be a sudden drastic change of personality.'

Malcolm suppressed a remark as heroically as he
had suppressed the yawn. 'Well, anything you want?
Anything you need?'

Charisma smiled and shook his head. Then, as if
offering them a token of gratitude, he said: 'One thing
you might like to know. It's all over between me and
Donna.'

This livened them up. Sicknote and Kevin looked at
Malcolm and grinned, now only too happy to listen for
a few minutes longer.

'You mean she's not living at your place no more?'
Kevin prompted.

'No. Finished. All quite amicable and civilized.'

Sicknote looked incredulous. 'You just said "Move out", and she moved?'

'Got no reason to be round at my gaff any more, has she? Not now it's all over between us.'

Malcolm felt a flicker of unease. Of course it might be that Donna had found Charisma to be a dead loss even before his injuries, and now she was glad of an excuse to write him off. But it was unlike her to retire gracefully from the scene – any scene. 'Amicable' and 'civilized': they weren't words you associated with Donna. When she had moved in with Liver Salts he had had to take her to court to get rid of her, and even then she got half of everything he had. Malcolm shifted in his chair.

'Don't worry about me, lads,' Charisma went on breezily. 'I made it quite clear to her that I wanted her to vacate my place before I got out of hospital. I can look after myself. There's no flies on me.'

His three visitors exchanged glances and set up a mocking sound of 'Bzz, bzz, bzz' in unison. Charisma laughed. He obviously thought they were a right lot of cards, his mates.

It was a relief to quit the bedside and head for home. The next morning the three of them took pleasure in spreading the news of Charisma's gallant stand for freedom; but less pleasure in the sceptical glances which confirmed their own suspicions that the whole thing sounded too pat and easy.

There were other things to concentrate on, such as George Green and the boxing contest. He had to be talked into agreeing to fight.

As senior fireman, Malcolm was leaned on to keep the pressure up. He could not officially order Fireman Green to take part in the area tournament. But he could deliver some pinpricks of guilt in an effort to shame him into it. It was worth a try.

News that had just come in from Jaffa provided a good beginning.

'All the other areas,' Malcolm pronounced reproachfully in the Locker room, 'are putting in a challenger. All except our little lot. Even South-East have been able to find a contender to challenge Conker Coburn.'

George slammed the door of his locker. 'It's not on, fellas.'

The others stared at him as if trying hypnotism. 'Didn't you used to know Kurt Winger?' Vaseline winked. 'They tell me he's the north-east's contender. Used to be called Stinger Winger. Never did know why.'

George rose to the bait. 'Well, it's because he comes at you with these fast, stinging flurries.' He could not resist a demonstration. He danced towards Sicknote, who managed to keep as still as a monument while George threw lots of little punches around his head, making sure none of them landed. 'The danger is that he's got fast hands. He works away at the eyes and the cheekbones. Clever stuff.'

'Pretty tough opposition?' insinuated Malcolm.

'Nah. He's got a glass jaw. One good shot on the button and it's goodnight, nurse.'

'He's a friend of yours?' Tony asked innocently.

'Loves me like a brother. Twice I've broken his jaw, and twice I've put him out for the count.'

'Which shows,' said Malcolm, 'what a terrific contender you could be.'

Everyone applauded.

'Leave it out. About a century ago, maybe.'

'Now look, George. If there aren't four boxers to compete, there can't be a contest. No contest, no money. Someone who needs a kidney machine might die.'

The rest of them were quick to pick up the theme.

'Some kid who needs an operation might never walk again . . . some old folks in the twilight of their lives, looking forward to seeing the sea just once more before they die . . . help for victims of a fire – God knows we've seen enough of *them* and what it's like for them afterwards . . .'

Malcolm said: 'George, it's your duty.'

'Frankly, I don't know how I'd live with my conscience if it was me.' Tony's voice was as dark as his face.

'Guide dogs for the blind,' added Kevin.

'Oh, bloody hell.' George's shoulders sagged in defeat. 'All right.'

They were all cheering as the bells went down.

Station Officer Tate had just tossed back a couple of aspirin as his sub officer appeared in the doorway. 'A flat fire. High rise.' Hallam stopped and leaned forward. 'You all right, guv?'

'Why shouldn't I be all right?'

'I reckon you'd be better off giving it a miss today. You honestly don't look up to it.'

'You suddenly got medical qualifications?'

'No, guv, it's just that – '

'When I want your opinion about whether or not I'm fit to be on watch, I'll ask for it.'

They raced down to the Appliance room, where Josie and Vaseline were dragging on their gear and heading for the pump ladder. Malcolm glanced at Josie's mouth as she passed.

'You look as though you've already gone two rounds with Conker Coburn.'

'It's just a cold sore. It's going now.'

'That ain't a cold sore.' Vaseline was climbing into the cab. 'It's a love-bite.'

'You'd know the difference, would you?'

'Let's put it this way,' he leered. 'You'd know the difference if I'd given it to you.'

Tate felt his knees shaking. It was crazy. This shout was not going to be any different from hundreds of others. But he was finding it difficult to force his legs to carry him towards the appliance. He clasped his hands together to squeeze confidence back into himself. He knew every routine that might be called for. He had seen it all before, he knew what to do in any possible circumstance. It would all be done according to the book and then it would be over, and they could get back to the station and chalk up another successful operation.

He was still haunted by the memory of that sweatshop fire; the faulty engine, the delay that had cost lives. He willed this engine not to splutter and give out on them.

There were no hitches. They were at the scene within six minutes. Smoke was curling out from a window on the eighth floor of the high rise block. A neighbour who had reported the outbreak sounded suitably shocked and distraught as he bustled forward to add anything the fire officers might want to know; but at the same time he was hoarding up the experiences and emotions so that he could indulge himself at length in the pub, or in court, or wherever he had a chance to hold forth.

'I'll bet it was paraffin,' he babbled. 'That old Mrs Emerson and her daughter Rita, their electricity's been cut off, the way I hear it. But if they can't afford the electric, where'd they get the money for the paraffin? And anyway they didn't ought to be allowed paraffin heaters in a place like this.'

Within the lobby the lift descended and disgorged a huddle of worried residents. Tate stamped forward to wave them out of the way. Hallam was following with the pump ladder team.

'You take us up, Kevin,' said Tate, 'then stay in the lift. Communications man.'

'Right, guv.'

Before the door slid shut, Tate looked back to make sure preparations were going ahead fast. Bayleaf and the pump crew at the side of the building were preparing to charge the dry riser while Josie and Vaseline hauled a hose towards it. Hallam had unlocked the fire box in the lobby and thrown the fire switch to the 'On' position before squeezing into the lift.

The door slid shut and they went up to the eighth floor.

Far below, Bayleaf was attempting to charge the dry riser from the pump. But he could feel no pressure. A glance at the gauges confirmed his worst fear. He yelled at Vaseline, by the fire brigade inlet: 'I'm pumping against no head.'

George and Sicknote were putting on their breathing apparatus as they emerged on to the eighth floor landing. They began smashing down the door of the flat from under which black, acrid smoke was gushing. Hallam hurried to the dry riser inlet; then turned back in horror.

'Guv, the bloody outlet's been vandalized.'

Tate felt as if he had been kicked in the stomach. He had sensed that this shout wasn't going to be a routine job, but this was outright nightmare. He stumbled forward as George and Sicknote staved the door in and began to edge their way through the billows of smoke which this released. They were looking back for the expected water. All they were offered was Tate's yell, 'Some bastard's vandalized the outlet!' He swung towards the balcony rail and leaned over. 'Someone down there – check that inlet.'

'This one's been knackered and all, guv,' came Tony's furious response.

The only thing for it was to haul the hose bodily up the stairs.

Another station's appliance had arrived on the scene. Two of its members, dressed in breathing apparatus, were brought up by Kevin to join George and Sicknote in the flat. Flame abruptly licked out at them from an inner door. Sicknote groped for a fire extinguisher on the wall, but his attempts to douse the flames with it were useless. He and George plunged on through a door into the heart of the blaze.

Intermittently through the swirl of red tongues and foul smoke they could glimpse two figures in the inferno of the room. An old woman was crouched over the sprawled body of a younger one. Mrs Emerson was just conscious, but too feeble to lift her unconscious daughter from the couch. She looked over her shoulder at what must have seemed like horror film figures in their B.A.s clumping towards her. George lifted her to her feet and passed her to Sicknote, who took her full weight. On his knees, George took off his face mask and gave Rita a quick fix of oxygen. She stirred, coughed raucously, and tried to claw her way upright. George put his mask back on his face, lifted her in his arms, and followed Sicknote through a sudden uprush of flame.

They stumbled out into a mist of smoke, which was so much thinner than the choking fog inside they could almost believe it was broad daylight. As the two women were laid carefully on the balcony, well away from their shattered front door, four more firefighters came lugging hoses up the stairs from the lower landing. At last it was possible to pump water into the flat.

Adding his weight to the team hauling on the hose, Tate had thrown in every last ounce of effort. His heart was pounding and he had difficulty in not sobbing aloud. Stooping over the hose and then standing up, he swayed against the wall.

175

Hallam put out a hand to steady him. 'Okay, guv? It's all right, we're winning.'

Tate pushed his sub's arm away. He was sick at heart; and he stayed that way even when the job was wrapped up and they were back at the station. He had had a bellyful. For once he had no word of commendation for any of his Watch. No word about anything, or anybody.

Josie stood wearily at the bus-stop wondering when the next bus would condescend to come along. She was getting cheesed off with this. It was so typical of Gerry to borrow her car and then somehow forget to bring it back. She stared down the road which was smeared a sour yellow from the sodium lighting, and mentally urged some red monster to swing round the corner way down beyond the traffic lights; and by a red monster she didn't mean a fire engine.

'Want a lift?'

Instinctively she stepped back a pace. The last time she had accepted a lift from a man the results had been catastrophic. But when she saw Bayleaf leaning quizzically out of his ageing Escort, she did not even pretend to hesitate. Thankfully she slid in beside him.

They had gone some distance before he said: 'I tell you, I wish I could get my hands on whoever vandalized that dry riser.'

'Makes you feel some folk are the lowest form of life, doesn't it? Makes you ashamed to be a human being.'

'What would you like to be if you weren't a human being?'

'I don't know. But something with only a very rudimentary nervous system.'

'Like an earthworm?'

They were laughing companionably as he stopped outside her front gate, and the weariness was slipping away from her. When she opened the car door she remembered David and his excuse for coming indoors with her. Bayleaf was not attempting any sort of excuse.

She said: 'Time for a cuppa?'

'Thought you'd never ask.'

In the kitchen she flopped down on to a chair and kicked off her shoes before heading for the sink to rinse some cups. Bayleaf was ahead of her, quiet and efficient and unfussy as ever. Leaning across him, she filled the electric kettle. Their elbows brushed together.

Awkwardly he said: 'Look, I don't know how you're fixed, but I've got a date with a boil-in-the-bag curry I could easily break.'

Their eyes met. If he had been the one to make a pass, would she have fought him off? Would she fight him off now? She sucked her lip, and the sore throbbed under her tongue.

'No problem,' said Bayleaf quickly. 'You've probably got a date. I'll swallow my cuppa and push off.' He was trying not to look at her mouth.

'It's not what you think.'

'None of my business, is it?'

'Look,' said Josie tautly, 'I almost got raped here last night, with a bit of a beating-up into the bargain. I turn up at work, and you and everyone else jump to the conclusion that it's got to be the result of a night of passion.'

She jerked away and went to collapse on the couch in the sitting-room. He did not follow immediately. When he came in he was carrying a tray with the teapot, milk jug, sugar basin and two cups and saucers. She did not flinch away when he settled himself next to her on the sofa. Staring straight ahead, she told him the full story, concluding with how she had reported it to the police and been told in a remarkably short time that the address David had given at night school did not exist and that

177

there was no record of any firm such as the one where he had claimed to be an accountant.

'You should have stayed at home today,' Bayleaf burst out. 'Rung in sick, or rung me. Or something. I mean . . .'

He ought to have understood that if she hadn't gone to work she would have been sitting here alone, asking herself over and over again if she had done anything to encourage that vicious little creep. And right now she was getting furious with herself, finding she was actually trying to make excuses for the bastard.

'Why do I feel guilty?' she wailed. 'Anyone would think *he* was the victim.'

Bayleaf put his arm round her. She could feel him tremble as his head rested against hers. His hand dug into her back.

'God, Jose, he could have killed you.'

He pulled her head round and kissed her, hard. Then kissed her again. She felt the sting on her lip but wanted it to go on. It took one hell of an effort to pull away.

'Mike . . .'

'Look, you know how I feel.' His breath was warm on her cheek. 'I'd do anything for you, you know that.'

'Oh, Mike, I . . .' She did not know how to finish or what she wanted to say or not say.

'I know, I know.' He got up. 'It's not on for loads of reasons, us being in the same Watch and all that.'

Josie gave a dry laugh. It was true. One impetuous move, and somebody guessing the truth, and she would never hear the end of it. Straight out of the Old Testament, when you came to think of it: daughter of Eve seducing mess manager. 'Mike, I don't know how I feel about you, because I'm not over Gerry yet. But one thing I do know, you love your wife and kid. You're lonely and missing them something awful now, but one day – '

'One day?' he echoed sardonically. 'I don't know. I don't know if me, Karen and Melanie will ever work out.'

'But you do want it to work out. And if you want it to, you'll make it work out, because you're that sort of bloke.' He was looking down at her with that wry puckering around his eyes that made her want to reach up and stroke his cheek; sad yet philosophical, perhaps too decent for his own good. 'Tell you what,' she said, 'if you could break that date with the boil-in-the-bag curry, we could go Dutch on a Chinese.'

He held out his hand to pull her up and kissed her again, this time very lightly and undemandingly.

Seeing his three mates sitting at his bedside had brought a lump to Charisma's throat. The lads were marvellous. Just off a rough old watch, and they had taken the trouble to come and see him. Charisma really loved them for what they and the guv'nor and Mrs Tate had done for him. He had been treated like a brother. It was at times like this that you really knew who your mates were.

Now that it was time to leave he wanted nothing in the world but to get back home to peace and quiet, and then get back to work along with that bloody marvellous team. He wouldn't make a fool of himself again.

It had been painful, telling Donna. He was proud of the way he had made himself go through with it. She had sat at his bedside and made some more spiteful cracks about Liver Salts, then said she was heartbroken to be let down by Leslie as well and he ought to be ashamed of himself. But he had stood his ground – or, rather, he had sat up straight in bed with his back firmly against his pillows – and he had said that there was no future for the two of them and she must pack up and leave. He hoped there would be no hard feelings. She had gazed blankly at him and he had feared a final explosion, but she had simply got up, patted his hand and walked off. As he watched her go he had felt guilty, yet at the same time cleansed and ready to start life all over again. It would never have worked, him and Donna. He was relieved that she had realized it too.

Being out of hospital was a wonderful sensation. They had been good to him in there, but it was great to be back in the real world again. He paid off the taxi with a flourish, and let himself into the peace of his home.

Only it was not as peaceful as he had expected. An odd buzz of voices filtered out from the sitting-room. He turned the knob and flung the door back.

The room was not very big, and certainly not big enough for the women and the equipment in it. Two of them sat with their heads under hair-drying hoods, while a third was staring at herself in a large wall mirror which had appeared in Charisma's absence. Donna, in a pink nylon overall, was putting tinted highlights into this customer's hair. All the remaining available wall space was festooned with advertisements for shampoo, perms and stylings.

Donna glimpsed Charisma in the glass.

'Oh, hello, Leslie. You should have told me you was coming out of hospital.'

Numbly he said: 'I didn't think you'd be here.' When she went on with her work unperturbed, he edged closer. 'Donna, could I have a word with you, please? In private.'

'Leslie, there's a little green bowl with peach tint mixed in the kitchen. Fetch it for us, would you, love?'

'I'm afraid I'm going to have to insist – '

'Leslie,' she said in a sizzling undertone, 'just do as you're told, please. I've got to have this lot out by twelve o'clock 'cos I've got three perms, an exhibition punk and a casual wave to do this afternoon.' As he tried to summon up something decisive, something that would somehow throw her and all her paraphernalia out of the house in one fell swoop, she changed to a wheedling tone. 'Please, Leslie.'

The three customers had all swivelled round to study him curiously. He could not stand the nosiness and the growing mockery in their faces. He went out and stayed out until he heard the last one leave. Then he came back into the sitting-room. Donna had flopped on her back on the sofa. She emitted an exaggerated sigh of exhaustion as he came in. He set about clearing away rollers, trying to get chairs back where they belonged and make the place look more like his home and less like a hairdressing salon.

'Leave that for a minute, Leslie. Just pop in the kitchen and put the kettle on for a cup of tea.' Before he could protest, she said: 'Oh, and while you're in there, can you fetch that little dustpan and brush, and sweep up that hair over there.'

He felt himself humiliatingly close to tears. 'Donna, I asked you to get out of my house before I came out of hospital. And all you've done is turn it into a . . . a . . .'

'Leslie, have you done anything yet about compensation from the Brigade for your injuries?' She swung her legs off the sofa and began to concentrate on peeling off her nail polish.

'Twice you came to see me in hospital,' he said. 'Just twice. And that second time I told you that you and me getting together was a bad idea.' It was no good explaining rationally to her or expecting sympathy from her. He had been lonely when his mother died, then Donna had come along and he had thought it meant happiness. It hadn't taken long to see his mistake. She had made a mug of him, and now he didn't want sympathy or sweet-talk or bitter argument or anything. There was only one thing in the world he wanted. 'I want you to go,' he cried. 'Donna, please. Just *go*.'

She studied her fingernails, sighed, and got up. 'All right, if it's going to upset you I'll put the kettle on and fetch the dustpan and brush myself.'

She pranced past him without looking into his face.

13

I N THE nightmare he was fighting his way through a quagmire of molten lava, his feet getting more heavily bogged down with every step. Sooner or later his boots would catch fire and his flesh would be fried. Somewhere he had parked the pump ladder, but he had forgotten where it was and knew that he had lost the parking ticket anyway. Some Indian girls were waving desperately from the top of a gantry, but the steps up to them had already been scorched away and still he couldn't remember the street or the multi-storey car park where he had left the ladder.

And where, for God's sake, was the water? He swayed towards the towpath of a canal, but it had been scorched dry.

Somebody was shouting: Sidney!' How could they know his name when he himself didn't even know where he was? 'Sidney!' Whoever it might be, she was very cross with him. She didn't understand that he was doing his best to reach her and put the fire out, but now his feet wouldn't move at all.

When it was all over, he'd be the one to get the blame. He was supposed to be in charge. It was his fault the appliance had gone missing, his fault that the high riser in the building hadn't been checked, which was why it was all on fire now, and his fault that he was getting too old and his mind was too shagged out to cope with decisions.

He heard a groaning and snoring in his own throat as

the smoke got to it. On top of everything else, he had forgotten to issue himself with breathing apparatus.

'Sidney!'

Tate dragged himself up through the swirling shapes and opened his eyes.

At the foot of the stairs Nancy was raging: 'D'you know what the time is?'

He tumbled out of bed and blundered towards the bathroom. His feet were still sluggish and he was not sure his legs would support him after all that trudging through liquid fire.

Washing and shaving quickly, he went back to the bedroom still in a trance, groping for his clothes. Where was his shirt? Where were his clean socks? He wanted to call down and ask Nancy, but did not dare. Going downstairs he found that he had to grab the banister rail to stop himself falling.

'And about time.' Nancy slammed a plate of bacon, egg and fried bread on the table as he reached the kitchen. 'I've been calling you since seven.' When he lowered himself on to his chair without answering, she raised her voice to a piercing rasp. 'A fine start to my day. Yelling myself hoarse trying to get you up and out of it.'

'You should have had a lie-in,' he mumbled.

'A lie-in? And then what would you have had to eat? You'd have gone on watch with nothing in your stomach.' She sloshed tea so violently into his cup that a gout of it splashed back over the edge, into the saucer. Clattering the pot down, she ran a hand through her tangle of dark hair, with its twists of grey strands. 'Then you get a few shouts, don't have a chance to eat proper until you get home, and what happens? You get an ulcer on top of everything else, that's what. Anyway, fat chance of me getting any sleep if I did have a lie-in. You'd get lost in space looking for your gear.

"Where's me vest, Nance? Where's me underpants, Nance? Where's me head, Nance?" That's what I've had every morning. When did I ever get a lie-in since you and me got married?'

Tate pushed his plate away. 'That egg's runny.'

'I turned it over like I always do.'

He swallowed his tea, scorching his throat, and reached for his jacket.

'Anyway, I haven't got time.'

It was true, but that didn't make things any better so far as Nancy was concerned. Her cheeks pouted as if she was about to blow a loud raspberry on a trombone. Then she snatched up his breakfast plate and dumped the lot, plate and all, into the kitchen bin.

'Maybe you'd have time to eat a decent breakfast, Sidney, if you weren't zonked out on Scotch every night. Showing up here every morning with a hangover that makes you look like the creature from the black bloody lagoon.'

He headed for the back door. His head was pounding just the way it had done yesterday and just the way it had gone during the nightmare. Something else he didn't have time for was one of his wife's tantrums. There had been too many of them just lately.

'I've told you, you should see a doctor.' She stepped in front of the door to block his way out. 'The way you're going on, it's not right. I don't know how you are when it comes to bossing Blue Watch about, Sidney, but do you want to know something? The last few weeks with *me* you've been no fun. No fun at all.'

Tate pushed her furiously aside and stormed off towards the garage.

He heard the back door slam really hard behind him but did not look back. Bundling himself into the Sierra, he revved furiously and accelerated like a maniac down the drive. At the junction he ignored the Stop sign which he had religiously obeyed for so many years. When he spun round the corner with a screech of tyres, a woman with a dog on the zebra crossing jerked back and he heard the faint wail of the dog. Tate raced away down the familiar avenue to the familiar roundabout where he met the main road. The directions on the large sign before the roundabout were familiar, too; so familiar that he had not bothered to look consciously at them for longer than he could remember.

Now he took in the names and road numbers. Automatically he signalled to turn right and began to move into the inner lane of the roundabout. Then the thought of showing up at the station to go through the deadly routine yet again, waiting for the next disaster and the next shudders of naked terror, bubbled up in his mind. He swung the car violently to the left, cut across the path of a pick-up truck which rewarded him with a blast on its horn, and settled to a steady, determined forty through the thirty-miles-per-hour limit until he reached the dual carriageway. There he opened up to seventy and then beyond, putting Blackwall Fire Station further and further behind him at an increasing speed.

Unlike the station officer, the sub officer was in unusually good spirits this morning. John Hallam had been half-way through breakfast when Sandra went upstairs to take a morning cup of tea to her father. Old Albert insisted on that cup every morning before he would contemplate getting up. It suited Hallam. Seeing Albert regularly across the breakfast table would have destroyed his appetite even more effectively than the apprehension of a difficult day ahead.

Today when Sandra came back she was still carrying the cup and saucer.

'Did you hear Dad come in last night?'

'No.'

186

'He told me he was going out with Edith.'

'Dirty old stop-out.'

'That's just it. He's still out.'

'That's why I didn't hear him come in,' said Hallam self righteously.

'But John, for heavens' sake, anything could have happened to him at his age. If he got knocked down on the way back, or mugged, or – '

The phone rang. They stared at each other. Sandra let out a shivering gasp and put the cup and saucer down. Hallam got up. If there was bad news, he would have to assume the responsibility of coping with it.

What he heard was far from being bad news. He could hardly believe his ears. Nor could Sandra, when he put the receiver down and turned gleefully back towards her.

'They've gone and done it.'

'Done what?'

'Left a note for the Warden of that old folks' home. Might at least have left one for us as well.'

'John, what are you talking about? Is Dad all right or isn't he?'

'Oh, I reckon he's doing all right. He and Edith have eloped. To Edinburgh, for starters – don't know if they're stopping off at Gretna Green.'

'Eloped?' Sandra looked dazed. Her heavy lower lip – the only feature in which she resembled her father – drooped. Then something occurred to her. She hurried upstairs again. When she came back she was nodding but still half-disbelieving. 'The old . . . old . . .'

'Old sod,' her husband supplied helpfully.

'All his clothes have gone. Packed the lot and sneaked out without me as much as noticing.'

'As long as he didn't nick any of my silk ties on the way.'

'John, oughtn't we to inform the police?'

187

'They're not exactly under age, are they?'

John Hallam set out for the station in a genial mood, wishing well to all mankind. He was whistling as he entered the locker room. This was unusual enough to provoke a sidelong glance from Josie, to which Bayleaf's eyebrows added a silent question. Hallam was delighted to impart the news that his father-in-law had fled with an ageing soul-mate across the northern border.

Bayleaf shook his head. 'Seriously, John, as a matter of some urgency I should inform Interpol.'

Hallam went up the stairs to the top floor two at a time. He was still whistling as he pushed open the door of Tate's office, expecting to find the station officer behind his desk and hoping he would be in a better mood than he had been yesterday.

The chair was empty. Hallam glanced at his watch. A couple of minutes to go, but the guv'nor was cutting it a bit fine and that wasn't like him. Hallam stopped whistling and went downstairs to see if Tate had in fact been earlier than usual and was already waiting down there for his sub to join him and take parade. There was still no sign of him; and nobody had seen the station officer.

Reluctantly Hallam phoned Mrs Tate.

She sounded agitated at once. Sidney had left home as usual, a bit later than normal, but surely in time for parade. Hallam got certain vibes from her tone of voice. Sidney had been held up, she hinted awkwardly, by a last-minute discussion on something they had to settle, and perhaps he went out a bit ragged.

The team had drifted into the Watch room and were waiting for his report. It was weird how telepathic you got to be when you worked closely with one another for such a length of time. They were like a lot of smoke detectors, sniffing trouble before it had even taken hold.

'He's on his way,' said Hallam. 'Got delayed. Maybe a bit of a barney.'

'Now, me and Jean,' said Sicknote, 'if we have a row we always try to patch it up before I come on watch, in case anything happens to me.'

'Looking on the bright side,' said Vaseline, 'I suppose there's just a chance you might choke on one of your headache tablets.'

'Or drown in your throat linctus,' added Kevin.

'All right, all right.' Hallam's early morning cheerfulness had drained away. 'Stop polluting the air. There's a working fire station to run here. Malcolm, give us a hand with roll-call.'

'Sub.' Kevin looked down at the open log-book. 'Should I make a nine o'clock booking saying the guv'nor ain't here for roll-call?'

There was a long pause. Silently Hallam consulted Bayleaf, and hoped that what he was getting was encouragement. He reached out and shut the log-book. 'Not yet. Leave it.'

Leave it. But for how long?

Roll-call over, they stepped out of their boots and arranged gear around the appliances in readiness for whatever got chucked at them during the Watch. Hallam's went in beside the pump, Malcolm's near the PL where on any shout today he would occupy Hallam's normal riding position.

Everything was neat and well organized, as it should be. Except for the absence of the station officer.

There must have been a smash somewhere. In which case it would be right and proper to record Tate's absence and tie it in later with a report of the accident.

Unless there was some other explanation.

Hallam was in a spot. According to brigade orders he ought, undoubtedly, to have entered Tate as absent from duty with no reason given, and reported him to

Area Staff. His own job could be on the line. Who was going to protect him if Tate failed to show up at all? This was a highly disciplined service. He could not go on much longer pretending the station officer was here when he wasn't.

Why the hell hadn't Tate phoned in? He knew the procedure better than any of them.

Warily Hallam checked with the Old Bill on possible accidents between here and Tate's home neighbourhood. He gleaned only that there had been one minor incident involving a cyclist in a road which Tate would never have been likely to take, and one a bit closer to home involving a drunk driver who had managed to be spectacularly over the limit at eight-forty in the morning. Hallam tried well-proven contacts in the local ambulance service and at two hospitals with which Blue Watch had become all too well acquainted over the years. Still he drew a blank.

Where could Tate have got to, and how could he of all people have neglected to ring in?

At nine-twenty-five Hallam gave up and indicated to Kevin, who was on duty in the Watch room, that he should open the log-book. Bayleaf and Malcolm watched in silence.

'Enter that the guv'nor is absent from duty with no reason given.' Grimly Hallam picked up the phone and rang Area Staff.

Bayleaf edged out of the room, patting him on the shoulder. Malcolm followed suit. They both knew that he had stretched it far past the limit. They were on his side, just as he had tried to remain on Tate's side. You stuck by your guv'nor on a shout, in an emergency. What was so different about sticking by him now?

Hallam doubted that Area would see it quite that way.

It was almost a relief for everybody to hear the bells go down at a few minutes to ten.

The scaffolding reared six storeys above street level. Six men had been swarming over it the day before, but today they had been temporarily shifted to other jobs. Only one solitary figure leaned out from the top platform, holding on to one of the vertical poles but seeming to tilt further and further outwards.

A woman screamed. For a moment the group of people peering up from the pavement below scurried to either side, expecting the man to come plummeting down. He checked himself at the last moment as if to tantalize them, and wrapped an arm more firmly round the scaffolding pole.

A police van on the scene was augmented by another. As the crowd thickened and began to seep forward again, the police moved them several yards along the pavement and began to cordon off the immediate area. Above the man swung out again, howling something incoherent before dragging himself back again. There was a moment's lull before he let out another howl. This time his words were clear.

'Lorraine. I want Lorraine, or I'm going to jump.'

The Blackwall Station pump ladder coasted gently to a halt by the kerb, no siren sounding. Tony Sanderson craned his neck in an attempt to distinguish the features of the man against the background of overcast sky. He must be about thirty-five, dressed in jeans and a donkey jacket, and might well have been any one of a number of men capable of working up there. But right now, lowering himself into a dejected sitting position on the platform, he looked more like some sad bird that had lost its way.

Malcolm headed for one of the police officers, followed by three of the Watch.

The sergeant did not take his eyes off the slumped figure high above them. Throughout, neither his expression nor his voice was optimistic. 'He's known to us. Billy Whitby, a builder's labourer. Lives round the corner.'

'Any reason for all this?'

'He's threatening to dive unless we bring his girlfriend to him. I reckon he means it.'

'Can't you get her here, then?' asked Sicknote.

'That'd be a bit difficult. She's dead.' The sergeant looked away for a moment and cocked his head towards a woman of about thirty at the front of the group. She was huddled up in an old coat and had a pair of worn carpet slippers on her feet as if she had just got out of bed and grabbed the first things available. 'That's his sister.'

The woman heard her name and took it as a summons. She ducked under the tape of the cordon and dodged past an indignant constable. Her arms were folded tightly across her meagre chest as if holding in some stabs of grief, and her face was pinched with anxiety and cold.

The sergeant indicated the firemen at his side. 'It's all right, Mary. They'll get him down for you.'

She sized them up with lacklustre eyes. She had come along to the scene of the drama but had already given up hope. 'He was driving the car when it happened.' She spoke in a monotone, dutifully explaining to the firemen what the police must already have known. 'The smash what killed her. He's brain damaged, our Billy. Keeps asking for her. I tried to tell him over and over again, but he just don't understand. It don't sink in. He won't let it.'

'Poor bloke.'

Tony went on staring upwards, trying to assess what they would be expected to do and whether it could be done.

Malcolm said carefully to Mary: 'How do you think he'll react when we go up there?'

'If he sees you, and she's not there for him, he'll jump.'

So it was a matter of making sure they were not seen. On that exposed scaffolding it was going to be tricky. Too much responsibility, too much risk, all to save the life of a nutter who wanted to be dead anyway. It was difficult not to think that if he had wanted to do away with himself it was a pity he hadn't done it nice and neatly before lumbering somebody else with the responsibility of stopping him. But in this job you didn't pick and choose your clients.

A police constable led Malcolm and the other three firemen round to the side entrance of the building. A service lift took them to the roof, and Malcolm made a cautious recce. From here they could just make out the back of Billy's head above the ornamental parapet. Scaffolding began half-way along one side of the building, leading to the desperate man's perch. Another walkway went round the farther corner. Where Billy was sitting, he could be approached along the side without his seeing them until they were almost upon him. From the other end it might be possible to make a dash if his attention had been distracted in another direction. The danger was that the other direction might be downwards.

'Right.' Malcolm had made his decision.

He and Sicknote would cross the rooftop and prepare to get over the parapet and on to the platform to Billy's left, while Tony and Vaseline would get as close as possible to Billy along the concealed edge – hopefully close enough to make a grab from the right. Whichever of them got a grip on Billy first, it was going to be a matter of speed, not to mention a good foothold.

From the far corner Malcolm leaned over and signalled to the police inspector and his sergeant far below. They were not going to risk letting off a sudden barrage of blaring sirens or horns, but two police cars began revving steadily as if to drive away, and by chance a car in a nearby street obligingly let off a repetitive car alarm. The noise was not the kind to startle the man into jumping; but enough, they hoped, to cover the sound of shuffling feet along the wooden platform.

Tony edged inch by inch towards the corner closest to Billy. There were only a few yards between them, but it might have been a mile. He looked down, and gulped. People who were scared of heights had no business being in the Brigade. But that didn't stop you acquiring a dose of fear after years of service because you knew so much more than when you joined.

He almost let out a shout when an arm came round his waist. 'What are you doing?' he whispered fiercely.

'Relax. I ain't planning an indecent assault on you.' Vaseline was passing a line round him and then tying it round his own waist. 'I just want to make sure that when you make a grab for him, I can make a grab for *you*.'

'Okay. But careful where you grab. Remember I'm married.'

A helicopter buzzed its way along the Thames. It was an unexpected bonus. Not only did the sound help to cover their wary shuffling, but the sight of it had attracted Billy Whitby's attention. He stared at it for a few moments. Then, dragged from his trance back to reality, he stood up again.

Malcolm and Sicknote had lowered themselves over the parapet when Billy became aware of them. Malcolm moved as calmly and reassuringly as possible towards him.

'Lorraine!' he screamed. 'I want my Lorraine.'

'It's all right, Billy.' Malcolm kept his voice only just

194

above the level of the background noise. 'She's on her way, but you'll have to be patient. We're here to help her so she can come and have a word with you.'

Tony and Vaseline crept with infinite care round the corner. Now it was no longer a matter of yards but of feet. Tony felt sweat dripping from the back of his neck.

'I need her,' Billy was ranting on. 'I need to speak to her. Right now. Where is she?'

Malcolm kept moving at his agonizingly slow, deliberate pace. Billy raised a protesting hand. Then something jolted him into looking round. He was a big man, and physically strong, but his face so close to Tony's was stained with tears, and his expression was that of a frightened, abandoned child. Then it contorted into fury and he sprang sideways to hang, sprawling, over the rail. His feet began to push him away.

Tony made a grab, and managed to get his right arm round Billy's waist. But the man's weight carried the two of them on to a precarious balance against a diagonal corner strut. Tony felt his grip slackening. There was no foothold, nothing to hold on to; but he couldn't let go of that wriggling, demented man. The rope round his waist began to cut into him. He heard Vaseline panting, struggling to hold the two of them, one arm wrapped round a vertical scaffolding pole, taking all the strain.

Malcolm and Sicknote moved in fast now. They rushed to the corner, clutched the rope, and with one mighty heave got Billy and Tony back on to the narrow platform. Just as Malcolm was about to haul Billy away from the edge and pin him to the parapet, Billy lashed out with his left foot and kicked Tony clean off the platform. For an eternity Tony felt himself dangling in mid-air on the end of the rope, twisting slowly one way and then the other. Vaseline got both his arms round the pole and now held on while Tony groped outwards

with his foot and then got a knee on to the platform.
A hand took his, there was a last heave, and he was on
both his knees on the planking.

'Enjoy your trip?' breathed Vaseline.

Tony tried to cough up a smart retort, but all he could
manage was a brief, grateful grin.

The rest of the day was uneventful. Those who had
been up on that scaffolding were not complaining about
the lull. Tony Sanderson felt that a quiet afternoon
followed by a quiet evening at home was just about all
he could cope with right now. No more shinning around
scaffolding, and preferably no trips up the ladder.

When Red Watch took over, one of them brought in
an evening paper. Its front page was dominated by a
dramatic shot from the ground of Tony dangling from
the end of the rope.

'Typical of Blue Watch. Always hanging around.' But
the jibe was accompanied by a slap on the back.

It was dark as they drifted away across the station
yard. Tony headed for the bus-stop. Josie, whose
husband had still not returned her car, defied a
few raised eyebrows by unhesitatingly accepting a lift
from Bayleaf. Vaseline and George ambled towards the
Mercedes which George would be taking out later on a
few profitable hire jobs for his brother-in-law. He eyed
the large suitcase Vaseline was toting along with him.
An offer of temporary accommodation was one thing,
but this looked more like the beginning of a long stay.

Before he could ask Vaseline just how long he was
expecting the threat of vengeance to hang over him,
there was a wild bellow from the shadows.

'Hey! You owe me a ton. Come 'ere.'

Big Eddie emerged, a lot more substantial than any
shadow. He took on alarming substance as he charged
across the yard waving a roofing hammer. Vaseline let
out a panic-stricken yelp, dropped his gear, and flung

himself into the Merc. He had just managed to lock the door as Big Eddie arrived. Before George's horrified gaze, Eddie set about knocking hell out of the car roof and bonnet with his hammer.

'Lay off it!' George yelled. 'That's my motor!'

It wasn't, of course. It was Cyril's, which made things worse. But this was no time for complicated explanations. George hurled himself at Eddie, who had raised the hammer for an assault on the Merc's windscreen. Vaseline cowered even lower inside. George got a grip on Big Eddie's arm and dragged him aside, sending the hammer flying. Eddie emitted a wild roar and took a swing at him but missed. George swung in a right jab to Eddie's jaw, poised himself, and with a second terrific uppercut knocked out the big man, flat on his back.

There was a round of applause from Malcolm, Kevin and Sicknote in the doorway. Vaseline began sheepishly climbing out of the Merc to add his congratulations.

George was propped against the dented bonnet of the car, his right hand tucked into his left armpit. He stooped, straightened up, and stooped again as pain lanced through his wrist and knuckles. He knew one thing that was going to wipe the jubilant smiles off their faces. He gasped: 'I've busted me hand.'

Sure enough, their smiles faded as realization dawned. Any chance of him putting up a brave show in the boxing contest had just been written off.

Bayleaf had said nothing on the drive from the station to Josie's place. She knew she was going to ask him in. In spite of what she had said last time about Karen and his daughter, she only had to be close to him to know she could weaken. She was very ready to weaken.

When they came to a halt she let out a little moan. She had been cross enough about the absence of her car; but at this very moment she was sorry to see it back, knowing that its presence at the kerb just had to mean the presence of somebody else.

Bayleaf followed her gaze. Hunched over the wheel was Gerry. He was staring straight ahead as if he had all the time and patience in the world, which Josie bitterly knew he hadn't.

'Want me to hang around?' suggested Bayleaf. 'I mean, I don't mind.'

'No, you know what he's like.' She sighed. 'He'll create a scene and I don't think I can face that. Anyway, he's probably just decided to bring the car back.'

Getting out, she gave him a quick kiss, then braced herself to go and meet her husband.

He was climbing out of her car and watching the tail lights of Bayleaf's Escort retreating along the street. 'Oh, dear, I hope I didn't put Bayleaf off coming in?'

'No, he thought he'd have an early night. We're all pretty bushed, what with all the sex orgies and that.'

When they got indoors she indicated a few letters which had arrived for him. He riffled through them while she made two mugs of instant coffee. A couple of times he grunted, selecting a letter here and there and tossing the others towards the kitchen waste-bin. They missed but he made no move to go and pick them up. Gerry had never bothered to do that sort of thing; it had always been left to Josie to tidy up behind him.

She said: 'Gerry, why didn't you bring the car back?'

'I've brought it back. What do you suppose that is, outside?'

'I meant sooner.'

'I needed it. Got delayed.'

'And I needed it, too. I nearly got raped the other night because you didn't bring it back as you'd promised.' When his eyes opened wide in mockery and there were the beginnings of that clever-clever sneer of his, she explained in a rush. 'A bloke at Spanish class. Because I hadn't got my own car he offered me a lift home, and then he – '

'That'll teach you to venture into pastures new without checking out the undergrowth first.'

She could have knocked the mug of coffee flying out of his hand, but that would only have encouraged him in one of his sadistic little rages. 'You really don't give a damn, do you?' she said wearily.

'Do *you*?' He turned his attention back to the letters he had skimmed through. 'This all there is?'

'That's the lot. I don't have the address of your new bedsit.'

'Actually it's quite an old bedsit. Old and seedy, if you're really interested, which I don't suppose you are.'

'Gerry, why didn't you bring the car back?'

'I told you.' He chucked the keys into her lap. 'I needed it. I was looking for another job.'

'Why didn't you let me know?'

'Maybe I didn't trust you not to say, "Yet again?"' He put his coffee mug down and sank into that mood of whining accusation he was so skilled at. 'Anyway, you seem to have done all right. But then you women do, don't you? You've had Bayleaf ferrying you around, and you probably got a kick out of fluttering your eyelashes at this chap from the Spanish class – '

She launched herself across the kitchen and smacked him hard across the mouth. He touched his face thoughtfully, almost appreciatively, and smacked her back just as hard.

'See you around.'

Josie held back her tears until he had walked out and slammed the door behind him.

*　　*　　*

Tate had sat for a full hour in his car that morning before getting out and strolling aimlessly along Broadstairs promenade. The curve of sands in the arm of the bay below was cold and deserted. He leaned on the raillings for a while, staring at nothing. It was years since he and Nancy had brought the kids here. Now they were grown up, both of them had abandoned Broadstairs holidays in favour of the Costa Brava. There was nothing left here for him. Even memories were pale and blurred, with no warmth left in them. He could not understand why he had driven all this way, but still he could not force himself to go back. Not yet.

The tide was out. There was no rustle of waves lapping, no trace of a breeze. The only sound was the occasional swooping screech of a seagull. Then his ears pricked up. An ambulance was wailing somewhere along a road far across the town. Smoke curled up between two houses. It was only somebody stoking a bonfire. He resisted the impulse to go closer and see whether the man was taking proper precautions to avoid it getting out of hand and spreading to a neighbour's fence. The hee-haw of the ambulance faded and there was no accompaniment from police cars or firefighters.

At opening time he went down the slope to the Tartar Frigate on the quayside and drank a pint, followed by an early snack lunch. Still he had made no decisions.

There was a foul taste in his mouth: not of beer, but a sickness welling up from inside. He knew you could never rely on anything going smoothly in the firefighting game, but two things he had always hoped to rely on: apart, that is, from the lads themselves. Barring an act of God, an appliance would always get them to a shout fast enough to save lives; and once there, they would always be able to pump water fast enough to be sure of saving those lives. But he had been proved wrong. He smacked the table with his fist, and two customers at

200

the bar looked round. Wrong, he cursed to himself. The sweatshop, that blasted gearbox, and then the shambles over that dry riser . . . and what next?

It was late in the afternoon when he finally plodded back to the car. He drove slowly towards London, and even more slowly when he got caught up in the evening traffic. The closer he got to home, the worse he felt. He had let the lads down by not showing up, and next time there was a shout he couldn't be sure of not letting them down even more seriously. Every time the bells went down nowadays he got that pounding in his heart, that dry mouth, his hands damp with sweat. And every time he would go on asking himself what was going to go wrong this time, and the time after, and the time after that.

When he opened his front door, Nancy rushed from the kitchen and let out a shriek. He tried to stiffen himself against the shouts and recriminations he was sure were coming, and which he deserved anyway.

Instead she threw her arms round him and hugged him, and began to cry. 'Oh God, Sidney. I've been going spare.'

'Sorry.' It was all he could say. 'Sorry.'

'I've had the D.O. and everybody on the phone, I've had the station commander here. Where've you been?'

'Kent,' he said dully. 'Broadstairs.'

'Broadstairs? We haven't been near it for years. What did you want to go there for?'

'I don't know. Somewhere out of it, that's all. Anywhere out of it.'

And when they got round to it, when there was the inevitable enquiry, and the inevitable verdict, he was surely going to be out of it for good and all.

14

THE PLAN had seemed such a good thing in its early stages. When they sat around in the gloom of the flat, desperate for a solution to their problems, Robert had been proud of himself. The other two relied entirely upon him and he wasn't going to let them down. It was his chance to prove himself. He was a writer – with a name like Robert Burns, what else could he choose to be? – and he was going to prove that a writer not only came up with good ideas in poetry and prose but could put them into effect as well. A man of thought could be equally a man of action. A real-life robbery could be planned as coolly and satisfyingly as a fictional one.

It was Amanda's wretched pleas which had started it all, along with the tension which was too dangerously building up in her brother's erratic mind. 'Where's the baby going to be born?' Amanda had wailed; and Gary had squeezed her hand and glowered at Robert, demanding an answer. Robert was the one responsible for the baby; he was the one who had to come up with a happy ending. Rent arrears had gone on too long, and now an eviction order had been served on them. There was no money left even for food. Or even for paper on which to write the great political diatribe which Robert had been storing up in his head, ready for declaiming to group meetings and at television cameras once they had been lured close enough. Now there was a more mundane matter to deal with. The other two were relying on him to solve all their problems in one go.

It was early in the afternoon when they set out in the decrepit Lada, with its clumsily-sprayed green panel through which rust was showing again. The tax disc was already three months out of date; another of life's little luxuries which they could no longer afford. But soon there would be a new home, a new car, and some civilized food.

In the back seat Gary nursed the greasy brown holdall. His old anorak, black woolly hat and the holdall gave him the appearance of a plumber going out on a job – only it wasn't that kind of job.

Robert drove past the forecourt of Blackwall Fire Station. For some reason the yard was filling up with kids, and a couple of outsize figures in fancy dress were cavorting in front of the engines, out in the open on display. Glancing at a small girl hopping up and down with excitement, Amanda instinctively clasped her hands across her swollen stomach. Her eyes glowed with a kind of frightened exhilaration as the car turned at the next corner and headed down the side street towards the entrance of a builder's yard.

Amanda had worked for a while for a builders' merchant, and over the phone had had frequent dealings with this firm. It was from her inside knowledge that Robert had devised his tactics. She knew from things that had been said, and remarks her employer had made when the firm was dilatory in paying its bills, just how they operated and when the money was piling up at the end of the week. 'It's always the big ones who keep you waiting,' her boss had grumbled. 'They're always the last to pay up.' This time, swore Robert, they were going to pay up and there was going to be no waiting. A quick rush in, the money handed over, and then the getaway.

He parked close to the gates. He and Gary got out.

Now the moment of truth had come he felt terribly exposed. It was a long way across that builder's yard to the office.

Amanda had wound her window down and was staring an appeal at him with anguished eyes. He said: 'Just keep the engine running.'

'I know, I know. We've gone through all that.'

'It's . . . not too late to stop this, you know.'

'Bobby, are you going to get us out of the mess we're in, or aren't you?'

He turned and crossed the yard, with Gary trotting behind him. The office was up a flight of wooden steps against a side wall. At the top he paused, then pushed the door open and strode in.

The room was empty. Gary bumped into Robert and then looked around the place, his eyes suspicious and his mouth beginning to twitch. Turning to face a metal filing cabinet, he put the holdall on top of it and began to wrestle with the zip.

'It's stuck,' he whined. Within seconds he was tugging at the zip and snarling as if wanting to tear it open with his teeth. He was always too close to the edge like this, too ready to flip. The last time his temper had flared up, it had resulted in his spending two years in Rampton.

Robert swore. While Gary was still struggling, an inner door opened and a man in a grey suit came out. His hair was grey, too, and his face matched the general ensemble. He had all the marks of an accountant, just the sort of man a creative artist like Robert Burns most despised.

'Can I help?'

'Uh, well . . .' Robert glanced an agonized appeal at Gary.

'Who are you?' The man's politeness was fading fast. 'What do you want?'

Gary tore open the holdall and swung his sawn-off shotgun round towards the accountant.

Breathless, Robert said: 'We want the money.'

Gary jerked the gun to indicate that the man should hoist his arms into the air. But in spite of his alarm, for some reason the man had been able to summon up a weak grin. He obediently handed over the keys of the safe, and went on smirking while Robert pushed aside a few ledgers and fumbled wildly through the few papers that appeared to be inside.

'I don't believe this.' He groped right to the back of the safe. 'I just don't believe this. Where's all the collection money?'

'It was collected by Securicor half an hour ago.'

'What?'

Keeping a wary eye on Gary, the man nodded towards the desk. 'There's the petty cash box in the top drawer.'

So that was it. That was the lot. They racketed back down the steps, knowing the man would already be snatching up the phone. Half-way across the yard they met Amanda.

'What are you doing here? I told you to stay in the car and keep the – '

'The police. You know it's not taxed, and there's two of them snooping around.'

There had to be another way out. As a couple of workers in the yard moved away from the uneven swinging of Gary's shotgun, Robert spotted a door in the far wall. They began racing towards it, through and out into a dingy alley littered with cardboard boxes and strips of crumpled plastic.

'How much did we get?' asked Amanda eagerly.

'Twenty-eight pounds.'

'Twenty-eight pounds? You're kidding.'

'And a bag of change.'

'Oh, wonderful.' Tears choked her voice. 'Riches beyond the dreams of avarice.'

The distant menace of a police siren grew swiftly louder on its way towards them. It was approaching the end of the alley to their left. Robert broke into a run, leading the way towards the far end. He found himself a hundred yards or so from the back gates of the fire station just as another police car came into view at the junction beyond. A heavy lorry swung out in front of it, blocking the way for a moment or two.

'In there!' Amanda was yelling. 'Get in there!'

They raced for the fire station gates. Bobby was clanging them shut as the police car slewed round the lorry and stopped on the far side of the street. Two uniformed constables scrambled out and sprinted across the road. Gary glared hatred at them and waved the shotgun warningly to and fro.

The first constable came to a halt. 'Watch it, he's got a gun.'

'Two, actually,' Amanda jeered.

Bobby stared as she thrust a black pistol into his hand. 'Just a minute, you never told me about this. Where did you get . . . I mean, I don't know how to use it. I'm an artist, I . . . are you crazy?'

Not a word had been said out of place when Station Officer Tate, back from a week's sick leave, had resumed taking morning parade. There was not even a hint of sly, critical speculation about his future, though he suspected there had been plenty of that behind his back. If anything, Blue Watch had presented a particularly smart, well-disciplined turnout. The austere effect was ruined in the afternoon when Malcolm and Sicknote changed into their costumes and presented themselves for approval as a big red elephant and a yellow banana. Some of the black spots on the yellow costume made it look as if the banana was in an advanced state of decay. Since the occupant was Sicknote, this seemed appropriate enough to most of the Watch.

The coachload of kids with two teachers rolled into the yard, and the educational visit began – a beginning with some unusual features for Blackwall.

Tate waited until the visitors were steered into the Appliance room and the teachers had established reasonable hush. Then he positioned himself close to the pump ladder and cleared his throat.

'Welcome to Blackwall Fire Station, boys and girls. I hope you'll find your visit interesting. Just enjoy yourselves and ask any questions you want. One thing, though. Boys and girls, please don't mess around with any equipment unless one of us is supervising. It could be dangerous – right?'

'Right,' mumbled some of the kids.

Hallam stepped forward to take charge and divide them into groups. The men's wives, watching from the foot of the stairs, moved out of the way of the onrush and went back into the kitchen to make sandwiches and unwrap fruit cakes they had baked at home.

Bayleaf and Vaseline did a double job of explaining the workings of the appliances and making sure that no stray enthusiast attacked any part of the machines too vigorously. Some boys tried on fire helmets. Two lads who had shown a keen interest in the alarm system were suddenly grabbed by Kevin and hustled with mock severity towards Malcolm and Sicknote. As Welephant and Banana, they were hamming it up and amusing themselves marginally more than they amused the kids.

'So these are the two culprits, Fireman Kevin?'

'Two right little rascals, Welephant. They think it's a giggle to phone in false alarms.'

'Do you mean to tell me' – Malcolm manipulated his

trunk round in a threatening sweep – 'that two boys as bright as these two don't know that there could be a real-life emergency going on somewhere while we're being called out on a wild goose chase?'

'I'm afraid so, Welephant.'

'Then we'll have to teach them not to forget it, like the Welephant never forgets, won't we, Banana?'

'Got to get the message across,' Sicknote agreed. 'Tell you what' – he grasped Malcolm's trunk – 'I'll make it a trunk call!'

There was a wild hallooing from the top of the tower. It was going to be a noisy session, but the kids were a bright and agreeable lot. No reason why everything should not go swimmingly.

That was until the three strangers came panting into the yard. One man swung the heavy gates shut. Another was waving a shotgun to and fro as if practising spraying the façade of the building and anyone who got in his way. One little girl let out a pretended squeal of dismay. A boy with a freckled face and cheeky eyes clapped wildly, thinking it was all part of the day's programme. Even the howl of the police sirens added to the fun.

Nancy Tate saw the arrival of the three from the window of the mess. She knew this was no part of the day's programme. It looked wrong, felt wrong. She dashed up the stairs to her husband's office. The two of them went out on to the balcony above the yard, followed by Dorothy Sanderson and then a couple of the other wives.

'Bobby!' The wild-eyed young man with the shotgun was jabbing it upwards to draw his companion's attention to them.

The man called Bobby looked undecided about what to do next. Then he began shouting up at Tate, and across the yard at members of the Watch sidling in front of the children to protect them.

'Nobody move. Everyone just stay as you are and no one will get hurt. Nobody wants to hurt anyone. We're just . . . uh . . . do as we say and everyone will be all right.'

He was pacing to and fro, sizing up the geography of the station and the surrounding buildings, trying to look tough and determined. But Tate got the impression that he was desperately wondering what to do next.

There was a flicker of movement immediately below Tate. George Green and Tony Sanderson edged one step along the side of the appliances. Tate wanted to shout an order for them to stop. It was no time for mad gestures. But they froze as the creepy character with the shotgun spotted their movement and levelled the gun in warning. He looked as if he might enjoy firing it.

Bobby squared his shoulders to show that he could do his own bit of threatening and pointed the pistol in Tate's direction.

'You lot. I want you all down here. Everyone. Anybody left up there or in the building and . . . and there'll be serious trouble. Everyone down.'

Nancy Tate plucked at her husband's sleeve. 'Sidney, aren't you going to do anything?'

'We're going to do exactly what he tells us,' said Tate, 'until the kids and women are out of here.'

They filed downstairs, with Bobby waiting for them at the bottom. Out in the yard the girl was watching over the one with the shotgun, who kept waving it at the groups of kids and firemen. One of the teachers started a protest; but the gun steadied ominously and she fell silent.

'I want everyone in there.' Bobby pointed to the bay in the Appliance room. The children were herded through it into the Recreation room, joined in a few minutes by Tate and the women from upstairs. Bobby's voice grew louder yet shakier. 'That's it, keep moving.

All in there. Just stay cool and everyone will be okay. Keep moving.' Then, as Tate hesitated, he said: 'Hey, you. Are you the guy in charge here?'

'I'm the senior officer, yes.'

'Good. Those doors.' He was indicating the rear doors of the Appliance room. 'I want them closed. Closed and locked. And those at the front, as well. Locked – like *now*, all right?'

'Look, can't we discuss getting the kids and women out of here first? You don't need – '

'I'm the one who decides what we need. Just get busy on those doors.'

When he had obeyed, Tate joined the others in the Recreation room. Nancy looked helplessly to him for some kind of lead, some kind of guidance. He could have done with a supply of that himself. The odds were piling up against him again. A week away, to give him time to pull himself together, and the moment he was back this had to happen: something unpredictable, something that could not be dealt with by any practised routine.

George Green was still seething with the desire for action. 'This is ridiculous. What're we standing around here for?'

'I got the vague impression,' said Josie, 'that we're being held as hostages.'

'Well, stuff that. There's only three of them.'

'That's right,' said Vaseline.

'I didn't know you could count,' said John Hallam.

The jibe fell flat. What they didn't need right now were jokes.

Charisma said very solemnly: 'I think George is right. I mean, I've done a bit of karate, like. I'm for having a go.' He sized the others up cautiously. 'That is, if it's unanimous.'

Tony Sanderson groaned. 'All right, Charisma. You

banzai chop the geezer with the shotgun, and I'll over-power the girl. And Josie can take out the pretty one.'

'Look, Tony,' growled George, 'this is serious.'

'I know that. But we're not going to solve it by doing a Rambo, are we?'

Dorothy caught his arm. 'Don't you dare. Don't do anything stupid, any of you.'

'So what *do* we do?'

'I suppose,' said Vaseline, 'Charisma could charm the bird into surrendering.'

'I'm willing to give it a try.' No one could be sure whether or not he was serious. But now he was steamed up, there was no stopping him. He jerked his thumb conspiratorially towards the window. 'It might be possible to sneak the kids out of there.'

'Cross the yard, yeah,' Kevin contributed. 'Unlock the gates, and bosh, away we go.'

'Unless one of them goes out on to the balcony, they won't even see us.'

'Which isn't likely with the T. S. G. mob pointing rifles at them, as they're bound to be.'

Now they were all, like Nancy, looking at Tate.

Hallam said: 'Basically, guv, we're all for having a go at those loonies.'

'So am I, but the way you're talking it'd be too risky. Apart from anything else, one of them could poke his head through that door while you're in the middle of the manoeuvre. And what sort of reaction would you like to bet on? No, we see if we can get the women and kids out peacefully first. Without any aggro to them.' Tate stared into their faces, one after the other. 'Is that clear?'

It was clear, but not clear enough to work out how they were going to accomplish it.

By late afternoon the police had completely surrounded the block in which the fire station stood. The side streets were sealed off by cordons and police vehicles. Territorial support group marksmen had found vantage points in neighbouring buildings; one of them, ironically enough, on the top floor of the builder's warehouse, which commanded a good view into one corner of the station yard. A Scene of Crime control van was stationed on the corner, and there was an ambulance standing by. A trained negotiator, practised in the persuasion of talking people out of siege situations, sat waiting for first contact.

From a window in the first floor corridor, Amanda looked despondently out into the gathering dusk. Over her shoulder Bobby saw little pinpricks of light and brief reflections from weapons and uniform, a continuous shifting of shadows, the closing of strands of the net.

He stormed downstairs to make sure that Gary wasn't on the verge of doing something crazy. Amanda followed more slowly, carrying her weight heavily down each step.

'You all right?' When Gary nodded eagerly, happy to have so many people cowering under his control, Bobby went on: 'Listen. Amanda and I are going to have to stay upstairs for a bit. They could be climbing all over the roof, for all we know.'

Gary, always liable to change moods in a split second, looked less happy. His eyes flicked to and fro. 'I'm not going back,' he whimpered. 'Not to that place.'

'It's all right, love.' His sister put a soothing hand on his wrist. 'Bobby will think of something.'

Bobby was about to ask what sort of miracle he was supposed to think up, when a phone began ringing. He stared through the open door of the Watch room as the sound went on; and on, and on.

Station Officer Tate said: 'I think it might be sensible if someone answered that.'

Bobby looked helplessly at Amanda. She took charge,

213

snapping at Tate: 'You answer it. If it's the police, you tell them what the situation is and that we mean business.'

She jerked her head to indicate that Bobby should keep with her, close behind Tate as he picked up the phone.

'Hello. Yes. No it's Tate speaking, Station Officer Tate.' There was a pause. Bobby wanted to grab the phone, yell something decisive and commanding at whoever was at the other end, and issue more orders about the disposal of this man Tate. Or else lie down on the floor and let it all go away and prove to be just a bad dream. 'Yes,' Tate was saying levelly, 'two of them are beside me now.' He held out the receiver to Bobby. 'They want to talk to you.'

'Me?'

'You are Robert Burns, aren't you?'

'How do you . . . how do they know who I am?'

At his side Amanda said drearily: 'The car's in your name, remember?'

Tate was still offering the receiver. Bobby took it, felt it slipping through his damp fingers, and slammed it back on to its rest. He didn't like the way Tate was looking at him – almost pityingly. The bloody nerve of the man. It was insultingly casual, the way Tate turned away and went to rejoin the rest of his gang.

Bobby and Amanda trudged back to the first floor to keep watch. Not that they knew what to expect, or what to do about it when it came.

Amanda said: 'So where do we go from here?' Her fingers began twisting the ends of her black and white scarf, tightening it round her neck as if she wanted to practise tightening it round somebody else's.

He peered out. It was getting dark so quickly, and there was no way of going anywhere right now. Once Gary sensed that, things might get nasty. Didn't she realize what she had let them in for? All right, so Gary was her brother and they were both sorry for him and knew he didn't want to go back to an institutional tomb. But with all that lot waiting out there, he wasn't going to have much choice.

'Are you remotely aware of what we're up against? What do you expect me to do?'

All her impulsive passion was turning sour. 'You're supposed to be the bright one. The intellectual, the great undiscovered creative writer. You're the one who's got to come up with something dazzling.'

'Oh, I like that. That's lovely, that's really helpful and supportive. If you and your lunatic brother – '

'He's not a lunatic.'

'If you two,' he ploughed on, 'hadn't squandered every penny we'd got – every penny *I'd* earned – '

'"I absolutely refuse to allow us to become victims of a government conspiracy",' she quoted mockingly, '"to divide the nation into the haves and have-nots" . . . etcetera, etcetera. What about that little speech?'

'All right, all right. But that didn't mean I was prepared to act like some maniac terrorist threatening the lives of women and children, for God's sake.'

'Have I suggested that? It was you who was running around out there waving a gun about.'

He couldn't believe it. She had shoved the gun into his hand, and now she was condemning him for using it to intimidate people. So why had she given it to him? 'Look, you know I didn't even know about it. I don't know where you got it, or why you – '

'Don't worry,' she said. 'It's not loaded.'

'It's not?'

'Gary could only get ammunition for the shotgun.'

Somewhere downstairs they heard, faintly, a phone ringing again. It sounded like the same one as before. Bobby went to the head of the stairs.

'Are you going to answer it?' Tate was facing Gary along the barrel of the shotgun. 'You know, you or one of your friends is going to have to talk to someone, sometime.'

Bobby tensed, not daring to start a descent until he was sure how Gary was likely to react. Slowly, keeping the gun pointing at the station officer, Gary backed away. He was out of Bobby's range now, but presumably he must be lifting the phone. There was silence. Not a word. After what seemed an interminable delay, Gary came to the foot of the stairs and called, 'Bobby, Amanda.'

Bobby began hurrying down. 'What is it? What's up?'

'They know who we are, Bobby – the police – they've just been on the phone. And they know our names!'

It was no use trying to bluff. 'That's right, Gary. I'm afraid they do.'

'How do they know? How could they know that?' He was shaking, his trigger finger was unreliable.

'They just do, that's all.' No way was Bobby going to tell him about the car identification and how easy the rest of the connection would be to make. 'It doesn't make any difference.'

'I'm not going back.'

'Of course not. Once we've talked to them, sorted things out . . .'

Another phone began ringing, more loudly this time. It was the payphone right by the foot of the stairs. Gary jerked away as if he had been stung. Station Officer Tate was only a few feet away, watching and waiting. That expression of his was asking to be punched through the back of his head, but that would be no solution. Bobby knew that this time he had to resume command in front of the lot of them, before the whole thing fell apart. He lifted the phone, expecting to hear the sobering voice

216

of a police negotiator or else the less amenable tones of someone threatening a no-holds-barred attack.

Instead, it was someone asking for a Josie Ingham, someone claiming to be her husband. Some kind of put-up job? It made no sense. At a loss, Bobby left the receiver swinging from the end of its cord and looked at the faces in the far doorway, beyond the barrel of Gary's gun.

'Somebody here called Josie Ingham?'

The woman fire officer detached herself from the rest, looking just as unsure of herself as he felt.

'Says he's your husband,' growled Bobby. 'You've got two minutes to tell him you're okay. Okay?'

She brushed past him and picked up the receiver.

Gerry's voice was the last thing Josie had expected to come floating through this crazy melodrama. But it was typical Gerry, all right; frantically worked up and sounding almost accusing, as if she had no right to worry him like this.

'For God's sake, Jose, what's happening? I've just heard it on the radio. I can't believe it. Are you okay?'

'I'm fine.'

'They said there were men in there with guns. Is that true?'

She met Bobby's gaze and gave nothing back. Calmly she said: 'Yes, it's true.'

'I can't believe it. I don't know what to say.'

It was all so incongruous. She heard herself saying with bleak cynicism: 'Well, I suppose we could discuss the separation agreement, but I've only been given two minutes, so – '

'Two minutes? What's happening? What's going on?'

'You know what's going on. You've just told me you heard it on the news.'

'What did you mean, two minutes? Are they threatening you?'

'Not just me. But it's okay, no one's been hurt.' She glanced again at Bobby, this time trying to hammer home a message to him. 'They don't want to hurt anyone. It'll be all right.'

'Look, I'm coming down there.'

'Gerry, there's nothing you can do.'

'I can't just stand here and do nothing. I'm coming down.'

She hung up, and gave Bobby a curt nod as she went back to rejoin the rest of the Watch.

In the middle of the group, shielded from Gary's gaze, Hallam had pulled a couple of the schoolboys in closer and was saying, 'Guv, found this.' He held out one of their small Evac transmitters. 'One of the kids had it. Must've nicked it out of an appliance chill box.'

'I wasn't going to steal it, honest I wasn't,' pleaded the smaller boy. 'I only wanted to show Freddie, honestly.'

'Don't worry, sonny.' Tate looked down with dawning hope. 'You may have done us a very good turn. This could come in handy – very handy.'

15

IN THE confined space of the S.O.C. vehicle the
assistant district officer was growing impatient. One
thing Superintendent Hanson, the trained negotiator,
knew to be fatal was impatience. Twice he had begun
his careful, man-to-man appeal in a reasonable tone of
voice, and twice the target at the other end had hung up
on him. That was nothing unusual. It had taken a long
time at the West Wharf siege before he had managed
the exchange of even a few words, and most of those
from the other end had begun with insults. You stayed
calm and friendly, even with your own blood pressure
mounting by the minute; and left the bad language until
it was all over.

On the second attempt he had thought he might be
getting somewhere. There had been no response other
than a hiss of unsteady breathing, but at least someone
was there at the other end, taking it in. 'Hello. Can
you just acknowledge that you are there and can hear
me?' He kept it very level and conversational. 'Is
that you, Robert?' No reply. 'Is it Amanda . . .? Or
Gary?' He heard the breathing quicken for an instant,
and exchanged a hopeful glance with the Commander
leaning over him. 'Well, whoever it is, do you think we
could just talk for a minute? See if we can't find a way
out of this problem. That's not too much to ask, is it?
You know, just talk awhile . . .' The phone was hung
up, and he could not restrain a muttered 'Sod it'.

Give it five minutes and try again – and again, and

again – until someone at the other end cracked, but not so violently that one of the guns went off.

Each five minutes felt like a lifetime. Hanson took a deep breath, praying that this time there would be a response, and once more lifted the phone.

'Hello, can you hear me? Can you just acknowledge that you're there and can hear me? Is that you, Robert?'

This time the receiver at the other end was not replaced but was simply left dangling off the hook. Ultimately they might have to use the loud hailer. Not much chance of a man-to-man chat that way.

The officer in the corner was leaning excitedly across. 'Sir, I've got Station Officer Tate.'

'How the hell – '

'On the Evac, sir.'

There was a tense hush in the vehicle. Tate was keeping his voice down and rattling quickly through what he had to tell them. Both Hanson and the Commander followed his descriptions on the sketch layout of the fire station tacked to the wall of the van. They tried to visualize the hostages crammed into the Recreation room, with Tate on his knees under cover of the snooker table, Gary covering its door and at the same time trying to keep an eye on the corridor in case a break-in was attempted. And the other two? Apparently they were trying to blot out the windows with layers of Windolene. Pathetic stuff, thought Hanson; smearing over the glass wasn't going to save them if an all-out attack had to be launched. But if they were lulling themselves into a sense of false security, so much the better.

When Tate had finished, the Commander reached over and took the Evac. 'Right, Mr Tate. Nice work. Now, here's what *we* know. From your descriptions the one with the shotgun is called Gary Woods. Has a record of instability and violence. The girl's his sister.

The other man, Robert Burns, is her boyfriend. No known form on those two. From what we've managed to gather there's nothing to suggest we wouldn't be able to reason with them *if* we could just get a dialogue going. Remember, though, to be very careful with the brother. Understood?'

'Understood.'

'If you can't persuade them to talk to us, you and the rest of the Watch will have to do whatever you can to get them to see reason. And don't forget, we've got the phone in the Watch room on a direct line. All you or they have to do is pick it up, and we'll be here.'

'Hold it. I think one of them is . . .' Then there was abrupt silence. The group in the S.O.C. vehicle could only hope that Tate had hidden the Evac in time. All they could do now was go on waiting.

Bobby peered out through a spyhole he had left in the Windolene coating in Station Officer Tate's office. A couple of lights winked at him. In the darkness he could see nothing definite, yet the whole area out there seemed to be seething with life.

Amanda said flatly: 'You're going to have to deal with them at some point.'

'I know that. When I can think up a plan – '

'What's to plan? You tell them we want transport, a car, and guaranteed safe passage out of here. Or else you start shooting people.'

'Shooting people? Are you crazy? I'm not going to shoot people – especially with an unloaded pistol. Which I wouldn't know how to use even if it was loaded.'

'They don't know that. And what about Gary? His gun's loaded all right, and he doesn't intend going back to Rampton. And,' she said fiercely, 'I don't want to have our baby in Holloway.'

He touched her arm, and for a moment there was a

glow of the old tenderness between them. She forced a helpless smile and he knew he had to prove something to her: that he was still in charge, that there was a sane and safe way of getting out of all this, and that he could win their besiegers round. They wanted to talk reasonably. Okay, let them listen to some reasonable talk.

He said: 'For a start, I think we should let the kids go. They're only in the way, and even Gary would hardly start shooting kids.'

Amanda looked dubious but finally nodded in agreement. They went down to the Appliance room, which Gary was fitfully covering in the intervals between glaring at the huddle of women, children and firemen.

The station officer detached himself from the rest and came to meet the two of them.

Bobby said: 'We've decided to let the kids go.'

If Tate was surprised, he managed not to show it. 'That's a good start,' he said non-committally, then added: 'What about the women?'

Bobby looked at the tense, pleading faces above the children's heads. Scaring the daylights out of a few drabs like that was no fun, and no practical use. 'Okay,' he conceded, 'and the women.'

Amanda flared up. 'You never said anything about the women. They're our ticket out of here.'

'Will you be quiet for a minute and let me handle this? That's what you want me to do, so I'm doing it, right?'

She glared at him and went to stand beside her brother.

Tate said in that same deadpan manner: 'You're going to have to inform the police of your intentions.'

'Okay, okay. You got their number?'

Tate waved towards the Watch room. 'It's a direct line. You just pick it up and you'll find them on the other end.' As Bobby took a step towards him, suspicious of all this neat and tidy knowhow, Tate said: 'I've been in siege situations before. It's the usual procedure.'

'It is?' He ought not to have given away his own uncertainty. Quickly he blustered: 'Right, you do the talking. I'll tell you what to say. Tell 'em to stand well back while the women and kids come out. Any attempt to rush us or act silly, and Gary here starts picking off your men one at a time – or all in a rush, depending.'

He listened to every word of Tate's explanations over the phone, and when the Appliance room doors were opened just wide enough to let the hostages out in single file he stood close to the exit, scanning the rooftops across the road and catching glints of light on rifle barrels in upper windows.

The pistol jutted from his right hand, jerking every now and then to hasten the progress of a frightened kid out into the open. The coach which had brought them here now gathered them up. Waiting policemen escorted the women a few yards down the street to the nearby pub, which had by now been commandeered for the evening.

Then there was a hold-up. The firewoman whom Bobby had called to the phone a little while ago, Josie Ingham, was refusing to join the line of wives leaving. Tate waved her impatiently on. She shook her head.

'I'm part of this Watch, guv. If you lot have to stay then so do I.'

'She's right, Sidney.' Bobby could only assume that the dark-haired woman with the worn, darkly-lined face was Tate's wife. 'That goes for me too.'

'You're not part of this Watch, and you'll do what I tell you.'

'Oh, will I, now?'

'Yes, you bloody will.' Bobby had to admire the bossy old nit for the way he could make a command sound the

223

way it was meant to. 'The police are going to need to talk to one of us more urgently than the others to clarify the situation. So you're going.'

Mrs Tate gave him an affectionate twitch of a smile; and went.

And that seemed to be the lot.

Closing the doors as the coach drove off, Bobby went to join Amanda and her brother in the doorway of the Recreation room. 'We're moving upstairs. Let's go. All of you – get a move on.'

They began trooping up the stairs, along the corridor and into the mess, driven like sheep before Gary's prodding shotgun.

Once they were there, Bobby felt the reins slipping through his fingers again. The men were staring at him with contempt rather than fear. Only Gary and his wandering eyes seemed to worry them. And if Gary made a wrong move, turned away at the wrong moment or let himself be distracted, which one of them would make a grab for him? Bobby tried to make his pistol look as threatening as the shotgun. But there were too many men watching; he and Gary couldn't hope to cow the whole group if any of them got even a suspicion of a failing of nerve.

The fireman who had kept his elephant head on in an attempt to jolly the kids along and keep them from fretting now thankfully shed it and mopped his brow. 'Actually' – a right toffee-nosed type, thought Bobby sourly – 'if you think about it, I can't say I've ever heard or read of a case in the UK where someone holding hostages has ever come out the winner. You'd think there was a lesson to be drawn from that, wouldn't you?'

'There is,' snapped Amanda. 'Don't let the bastards beat you.'

The sub officer leaned with cold politeness towards her. 'Cigarette?'

'No, thank you., They're bad for you.'

Josie Ingham said: 'When's the baby due?'

Amanda hesitated. Bobby silently implored her not to fall for this phoney friendliness, but after a few seconds she said: 'March, since you ask.'

'What do you want – boy or girl?'

'Either, so long as it gets a chance to share society's cake.'

'That's easy.' It was the fireman with the broken nose who looked like a failed prizefighter. 'You work for it. You don't rob builders' yards.'

She stared. 'How do you know about that?'

Tate said: 'It was mentioned by the police when I was on the phone to them in the Watch room.'

'You should never have let him make that call,' Amanda blazed at Bobby. 'You should have done it yourself.'

'Doesn't make any difference.'

The fireman dressed up as a banana got his head free of the costume and said plaintively: 'I couldn't half do with a glass of milk. Ulcer's playing me up, you know.'

'Don't worry, Sicknote. Maybe you'll have it perforated with a few shotgun pellets.'

'What a card you are, Tony.'

'It's what they call black humour, isn't it, Toke?'

'Shut it.' Bobby could stand no more of this ribbing. He was sure it was meant to distract him while they planned something – but what? 'Shut it, right?'

'Actually,' said Tate mildly, 'I could do with a cup of tea.'

'Mine's a whisky and soda,' said one of the Watch, feigning to read a newspaper.

'What about it, miss?' Like his sub, Tate was trying it on with Amanda. 'You look as though you need some sort of refreshment as well.'

'Hey, Bobby.'

It was the first time Gary had spoken for ages. There was a tense hush as they all looked at him. He rolled his eyes towards Bobby and indicated that they should back away a few feet into the corridor. When the two of them were outside, he said in a shaky undertone: 'Look, what do we do, then?'

'I'm working on it, aren't I?'

'I mean, when we get the car. What do we do?'

'Well, we drive it away, don't we?'

'Where?'

'Where? I don't know. Away from here, out of it. We disappear. Leave the country or something.' Bobby made an effort to keep his voice from rising too hysterically. 'For God's sake, one thing at a time, Gary.'

The women were huddled round two tables. They had already had more to drink than they were used to, and it was not making them feel any better. After a few attempts at humour, largely concerned with this pub and the hours their husbands had spent in it before coming home, they spoke only in fits and starts, asking fragmentary questions that couldn't be answered yet. 'How long do you think they'll . . . what d'you suppose the police think they're up to . . . you don't really think that lunatic with the shotgun would . . .?' Every time the door swung open they all looked up hopefully, believing that this time there would be a message that it was all over and their men were coming out unharmed.

Dorothy Sanderson had chosen a seat commanding a view of that door and kept her gaze fixed on it. She was the first to see Gerry Ingham when he came in.

He summoned up one of those lopsided smiles that had never gone down with any of them, though at one stage they must have had some effect on Josie. 'Hello, ladies. Not the best of circumstances to meet again, is it?' He looked glumly around the bar.

Jean Quigley said: 'Josie's still in there, Gerry. It was her decision to stay.'

'I know. Some prancing twit in a uniform over the road told me that. Seemed more interested in the way I'd got through to Josie on the payphone. I got the impression one of his oiks had forgotten to keep tabs on it. In for a rocket, if you ask me.'

He bought himself a pint of lager without asking whether any of the rest of them wanted a drink and settled himself on a vacant stool beside Dorothy. He had taken three long gulps from his glass and was staring into space when she ventured: 'Sorry about you and . . . well, the way things have turned out.'

He still looked blank. 'Mm? What was that?'

'Just that I was sorry to hear about you and Josie breaking up.'

'Oh. Told you all about it, did she?'

'No, not in any detail, of course not. She's such a nice person. She was very good to me when I . . . well, had a bit of a problem. Very supportive, you know.'

'Ah, yes. Supportive. Is that because women have problems but men only have responsibilities, d'you think?'

'Look, I'm sorry.' Dorothy was flustered. She had only meant to be friendly, ease the strain a little. 'I didn't mean to interfere or anything.'

He studied her for a moment. Creepily she felt almost as if he was wondering whether to make a pass at her. 'No, I'm sorry,' he said at last, in what he must have thought was an appealing tone. 'It's just that all this . . . on top of everything else, you know . . .'

227

'Sure.' She could not resist asking, because she wanted it to be true: 'You must still love her, though?'

He went on looking at her in that weird way.

Bobby picked up the mess phone. Amanda had stationed herself in the kitchen and was covering the members of the Watch with the pistol as Bobby took a deep breath and announced his terms, trying to impress the occupants of this room as much as the negotiator at the other end.

When he had finished, the infuriatingly polite voice replied: 'I'll have to confer with my superior on that request, Bobby.'

'It's a demand, not a request.'

'Well, that's not a decision I can take.'

'So why am I talking to you? Why am I wasting my time talking to you?'

'Bobby, we're as anxious as you are to solve this problem, but we have to discuss – '

'There's nothing to discuss. I've told you what we want. It's simple. One, two, three – we get what we want, you get the hostages. There's nothing to discuss but when and what time.'

'It's not quite as simple as that, Bobby,' the voice droned on. 'We have to be sure of your good faith. I mean if, for example, you were to release some more of the hostages, then – '

'We gave you the women and the kids.' Bobby found himself shouting. 'What are you on about, good faith?'

'We appreciate your goodwill in that. It means we can work this thing out, Bobby.'

'And don't keep giving me that "Bobby" crap. You're no friend of mine. I'm not an idiot, do you think I don't know the games and tricks you people play? Given half a chance, you'll . . . we . . . we'll be zapped, right? You know what I'm saying? I'm saying that all we have is

228

these people. These are what's keeping us from being dead. So don't take me for a moron. I don't want bullshit and I don't want anyone hurt, either. Especially us. I have a very nervous friend with a shotgun here, know what I'm saying? So let's do this right.'

He slammed the phone down, hardly able to credit his own bravura performance. Neither could the rest, judging by the awestruck way they were looking at him.

'That's telling them,' said Amanda.

'Impressive,' said the sub officer stonily.

'Only one problem,' said Amanda. 'You didn't wait for an answer. Do we get the car, or what?'

As Bobby stared at the phone, not daring to lose face by picking it up again too soon, Tate said: 'Listen, son. Bobby – I can call you Bobby, can't I . . .?'

'Don't patronize him,' spat Amanda.

'I'm not trying to patronize anyone. I just thought as we're all, so to speak, in this mess together – '

'No pun intended,' said the toffee-nosed one at the mess table.

The station officer glared. 'In it together,' he went on, 'and probably for some time yet. So why don't we just talk it out, man to man, on a friendly basis?'

'We're holding you as hostages, for God's sake!' cried Amanda. 'How can we be friendly?'

'Well,' said one of the others, 'how about being just plain reasonable?'

'And being reasonable,' said Tate, 'is it reasonable to suppose that the police are likely to let you drive away from here? They don't operate like that. And it's reasonable to assume you both know that really. So where does that leave us?'

'Yeah,' said the black one. 'I mean, Amanda, what're you going to do – start shooting us and throwing us over the balcony one by one? I mean, are we just going to sit here while you do that?'

Amanda pointed the pistol at him. 'You've got a choice?'

'Amanda, look,' Bobby intervened. 'No one wants to hurt anyone here, okay?'

'That a fact?' said Josie Ingham. She pushed forward and confronted him. 'Who do you think you're kidding with all this Mister Nice Guy crap? You burst into this station waving guns around, terrifying women and kids, and then come on with this about not wanting to hurt anyone. Well, if you want bloody sympathy, you're not getting it from us.'

Before he could answer, Gary appeared in the doorway. 'They're out there, Bobby. They're coming round the back!'

Bobby sprinted up to the top floor, to his spyhole through the smeared window. Two shapes danced swiftly across the yard and vanished. They must be flattening themselves against the wall immediately below. He had no idea whether there was a side door there, or whether they proposed to smash their way in through a window.

Hurrying breathlessly back, he barked out orders. 'On your feet. We're moving out. To the top floor.' When nobody moved, he barked louder. 'Look, I'm telling you . . .' He turned and nodded Gary forward. The shotgun flailed towards them and Amanda came circling in from the other side with the pistol.

'You heard him. Move.'

The Watch were hustled upstairs and along the corridor to the General Office. 'And stay away from the windows,' Bobby commanded. 'No one goes near the windows. Keep an eye on them, Gary.'

As he led her back into the corridor, Amanda said: 'What are you going to do?' She was close to breaking point.

'How the hell do I know? It's what those bastards

out there are going to do.' He headed for the stairs, pounded down them yet again, and snatched up the mess phone. When the negotiator answered, Bobby wasted no time waiting for soothing noises. 'Listen, I don't want any more of that crap of yours. Anyone tries to get in here, and someone gets hurt. It'll be *your* responsibility. Get that?'

'No one is trying to get in there, Bobby. Just take it easy. I give you my word – '

'Your word's worth shit. Do we get a car or what?'

The door of the General Office was propped open. Outside, Gary fidgeted from one foot to the other. He looked apprehensively along the corridor and then back into the room. Inside, Tate felt his heart beginning to pound just the way he dreaded. He didn't want the Watch to see him break out in a sweat or notice his hands start to shake.

From the corner of his eye he was aware of George Green edging as casually as possible towards the filing cabinet just inside the doorway, sheltered from Gary's gaze by the open door. On the cabinet sat a black cloth bag. Tate realized at once what was in there: the cylinder of a B.F.C. extinguisher.

Gary was no longer framed in the doorway. Distracted by some kind of sound along the corridor, he was trying to keep both the General Office and Tate's office in his sights. And he had other problems. He moved away a few steps, and they heard his faint moan. 'Sis, I've got to go to the toilet.'

George grabbed the bag and the extinguisher.

'It's worth a try, guv.'

'It's got no trigger mechanism,' Sicknote pointed out.

Bayleaf indicated the desk. 'There's one in the drawer.'

By the time Bobby and Amanda appeared in the doorway to check them out, the team were lounging about trying to look as bored and gutless as possible. Suddenly Sicknote clutched his stomach and collapsed in a writhing heap on the floor. Bobby looked down indecisively. Amanda glanced back along the corridor as if urging Gary to get a move on.

George whipped the extinguisher out from behind his back. A jet of liquid lashed into Bobby's face. As Amanda screamed and launched herself into the room with the pistol, Kevin dived at her and slammed her against the wall. The pistol went flying, and landed at Vaseline's feet.

Amanda was streaming louder. 'Gary!'

Gary came pounding along the corridor and burst into the office. Every nerve in his body was urging him to fire the shotgun and rip the place apart. This whole thing had gone on for too long.

Vaseline raised the pistol. 'Don't do it.'

Gary aimed the shotgun lovingly at him. Vaseline pulled the trigger of the pistol, once, and then again. There were two clicks on the empty chambers. He froze for a second, then tossed the pistol aside and dived for cover behind the desk. The blast of the shotgun was a deafening roar in that confined space. Shattered glass from the window rained down into the yard below.

The thunderclap was succeeded by an incredible silence. Slowly Amanda stirred, pushing herself up from the floor. Bobby was wiping his streaming eyes with one hand and groping with the other for some way of hauling himself upright.

Gary stared from Bobby to his sister and back again, imploring one or the other to give him some instructions.

Amanda shook her head in defeat.

The message got through. Gary looked down at her

for a moment; then turned and shambled off along the corridor in the direction of the stairs.

Tate moved towards the door. Bayleaf put a restraining hand on his arm. 'No, guv. Don't.'

Tate gently removed his hand. 'Don't worry. Stay right here, the lot of you.'

He peered along the darkened corridor. There was no way of telling whether Gary had stopped just round the corner and was waiting, trigger-happy or trigger-desperate. He thought he heard a footfall, but any further sound was drowned by a few peremptory shouts outside the building and the sound of a revving engine. The shotgun blast had alarmed the spectators outside, and now there was another danger; they might come storming and smashing their way in and set Gary off again.

Tate reached the head of the stairs. No sign of Gary.

He went down step by step, with only pale patches of light through the windows to guide him, and a couple of those partially obscured by the Windolene. He almost allowed himself a pitying smile for the ineptitude of Bobby Burns.

On the first floor landing he headed cautiously for the Locker room. There wasn't really any other likely hiding-place along this corridor.

Before he reached it he became conscious of a slumped shape leaning against one of the pillars. In the gloom he could just make out Gary, down on the floor in an almost foetal position, knees up and his back to the pillar. The shotgun was still clutched possessively in both hands.

Tate took a deep breath. 'It's all over, son.'

Gary flinched and cowered away. His knuckles tightened.

'You want to give me the gun?' Tate murmured. He let the pause roll for an eternity of seconds. 'It'll go better for you if I can tell the police you volunteered it.'

A light that might have come from a powerful torch or some sort of spotlight that had been rigged up outside swept across Gary's face. Tears welled from his eyes and glistened on his cheeks.

'Come on.' Tate got a hold on the shotgun and drew it gently away between Gary's slackening fingers. He broke it open, removed the spent and unspent cartridges, and pocketed them. 'It's going to be all right,' he said gently.

16

THE POLICE had another job on their hands now. It was all they could do to stop the wives rushing from the pub to the fire station and hurling themselves into their husbands' arms, blocking the way as uniformed officers led the handcuffed Gary, Bobby and Amanda towards the waiting van. When the A.D.O. was sure the first hysteria of the reunions was over, he closed in on the station officer and Nancy Tate.

'We'll be hearing the full story in due course, I imagine.' He held out his hand. 'But the bits I've heard so far add up pretty impressively. Nice work. You should be proud of your husband, Mrs Tate.'

Revelling in the general hubbub, Tony Sanderson said: 'Not a bad act you put on in there, Sicknote.'

'Well, he's a natural to throw a dummy,' said Malcolm.

Charisma eyed Vaseline with a mixture of admiration and doubt. 'How did it feel, Vas? I mean, you know, when the pistol . . . um . . . didn't go off?'

'Only the laundry will tell the full story.'

Charisma grinned. It didn't take the grin long to fade. In all the panic he had forgotten Donna. Now she came back into his mind. Donna hadn't been with the other women helpers, and she hadn't shown up at the pub. He would find her waiting at home, probably moaning blue murder about him being late. Today's nasty situation had worked out fine in the end, but how was he going to work out this other one?

Josie and Gerry were the only couple who had not

thrown their arms around each other, hugging and kissing and talking happily, distraught nonsense. As he came towards her Josie had thought for a moment he might reach out for her; but once they were close it was as if he was sliding back into his old self, waiting for her to make any move there might be.

Stiffly he said: 'Josie. You all right?'

'Yeah, I'm all right.' She watched the police van door close on Gary, Bobby and Amanda. Somehow she felt sick – crazily – on their behalf. 'I appreciate,' she said with an effort, 'you coming and . . . well, you know . . .'

'Well, so long as . . . you know . . .'

It seemed that neither of them knew anything. They looked helplessly at each other. Then she shook her head and found herself walking past him, off into the night. She passed Bayleaf without turning her head.

'Don't worry, Bayleaf,' said Kevin. 'We've always got each other.'

Parade the next day seemed a bit of an anti-climax. Not that anybody want a re-run of anything like the previous day's events, but it would make talking points for weeks in the mess.

Tate determined that there was one other point that needed talking about, not to everyone on the Watch, but to the two he had always most relied upon. When parade had been dismissed to their duties, he beckoned Hallam and Bayleaf to follow him up to his office.

'I've got an apology to make,' he said bluntly. 'And I want it off my chest. That little wobbly of mine two weeks back – '

'Guv, you needed a rest,' said Hallam. 'Thank God you got one. Did you a world of good. How we'd have managed yesterday without you, I hate to think.'

'I let you and the lads down,' Tate persisted.

Bayleaf shook his head very slowly, very gravely. 'You've never done that yet, guv, and you never will.'

'I let you down. But not badly enough, it seems, for me to be suspended. They've had their enquiry, or post-mortem, you might say. I'm not being lobbed out of the service.'

Hallam let out an explosive gasp of relief. 'They'd be round the twist if they even considered it.'

'The station commander's been very decent about it. Came to see me and told me there wasn't going to be any witch hunt. "Sidney, you've given twenty-five years loyal service to the London Fire Brigade" was the way he put it, "and this is the first time you ever blotted your copybook." So it's written off. Forgotten. Except by me,' added Tate ruefully.

'Guv,' said Bayleaf, 'you *are* the London Fire Brigade.'